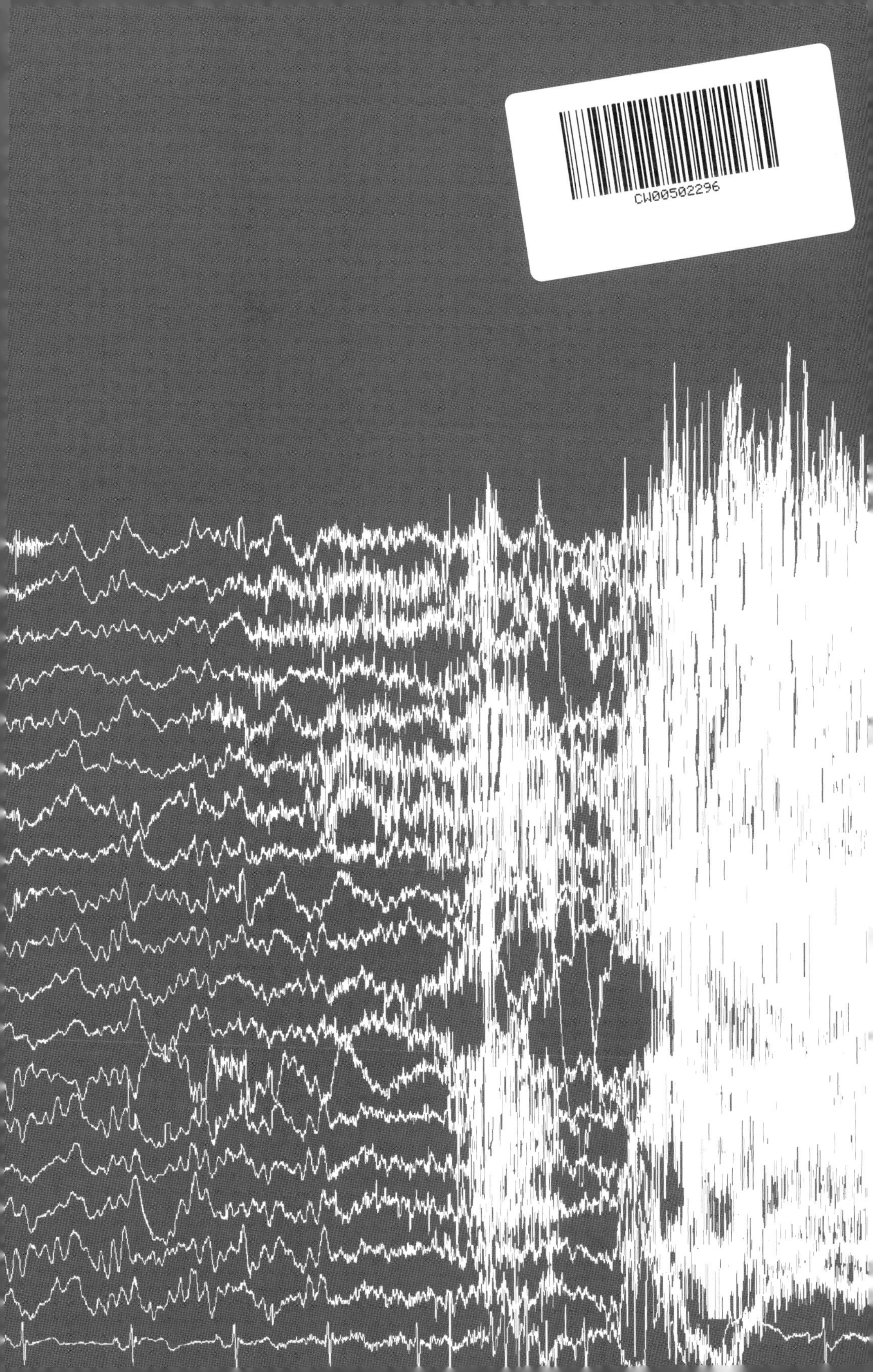
CW00502296

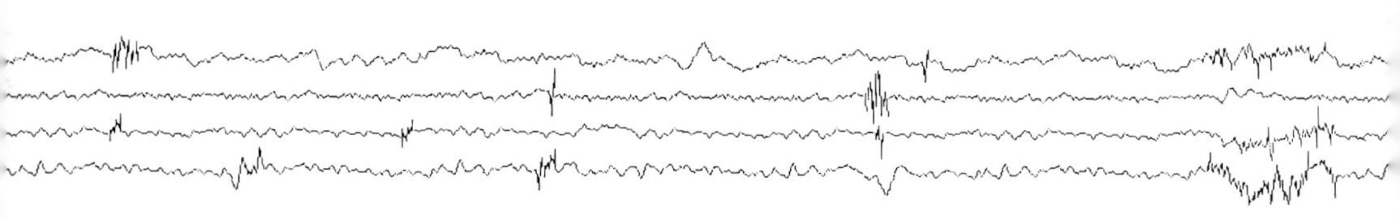

First published in the United Kingdom, 2016
by Forbes & Thomas
for the collaboration *Embroidered Minds*

embroideredminds@sandsthomas.co.uk

Printed by Short Run Press Ltd, Exeter, Devon

ISBN 978-0-9935052-0-1

EMBROIDERED MINDS of the MORRIS WOMEN

– A NOVEL –
IN SERIAL FORM

– PART ONE: *DON'T REMEMBER* –

wherein a tragic CONSPIRACY of SILENCE
surrounding ***William Morris's family***
is explored by

LESLIE FORBES

with JAN MARSH *and the artists*
CAROLINE ISGAR, SUE RIDGE,
ANDREW THOMAS & JULIA DWYER
Greatly assisted by various doctors & scientists
involved in **NEUROLOGICAL ISSUES**
(notably Professor Marjorie Lorch & Doctor Renata Whurr*)*

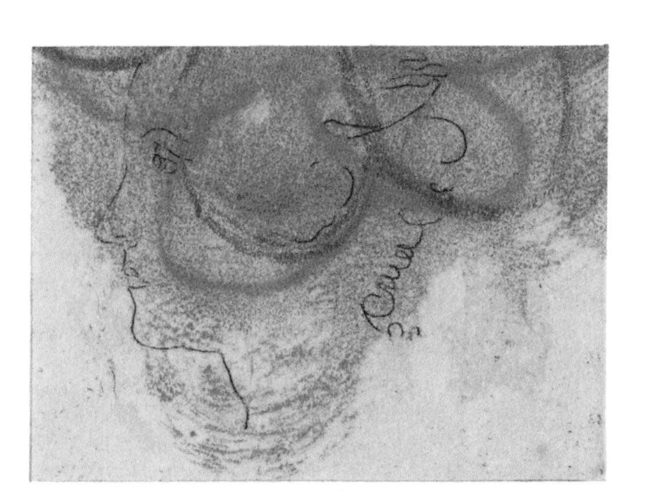

CHAPTER ONE

THE LOST RECORDINGS
(as transcribed in 1889)

1st Recording: *Jenny Remembers*
(Pertaining to the years up to and including 1889)

WITH YOUR WRISTS BOUND YOU CAN'T READ, so I made lists in my head, and invented stories to write later, hoping that the bromide and seizures wouldn't have faded my memory for good. I know that something terrible happened to me last year but when I try to remember my mind skips time, I am an emptying diary. Are you the doctor who unbound me? Lists of good doctors and bad get muddled with the recipes Mother keeps in a leather-bound notebook. *Doctor Spotted Dick and Doctor Peerless Pie-Face, Doctor Cobbled-nuts and Plum Foolish Pudding*. Papa's long, loving letters to me get lost in memories of his poetic sagas and his annotated fabric and wallpaper swatch books, or amongst the list of admirable reasons he gives for not visiting me: his experiments in dyeing as Art, his speaking engagements on behalf of the environment and the Socialist League and the Society for the Protection of Ancient Buildings. Mother is not yet ancient, but she needs protecting from me, because I'm like London Bridge, falling down, falling down, falling down, my fair lady.

'What is this doctor's name?' I asked Papa when you and I began our graphophone exchange. 'When can we meet?'

Papa told me that you wished to remain anonymous. He said it was best if we didn't meet face to face.

So your voice is all I have. My sweet companion, my patient perpetual Enquirer. *Listening* to me, not just recording symptoms. Every day you send two wax cylinders for the graphophone. On one are questions and answers from you, while the other cylinder - blank - is for my response. A miracle these graphophones are. By a neat mechanical contrivance they reproduce all our moods - humour, ardour, acidity, boredom, blood-curdling fear, eloquent silence. You must listen to a great deal of silence. I am a seashell held to your ear. Often I speak through voices not my own: the perpetrators of a crime, the conspirators, the victims too.

On your waxy cylinder you ask me a question: What was the crime?

Speak to the conspirators, the people who silence me. I hold my tongue, bite it many times, in fact, for how can one hold such a slippery thing except with one's teeth? Papa's rages, however, like his Socialism, are noisy. All our lives, the women in this family have done our best to soothe his roaring nature, which can be aroused even by the most inconsequential things. No one knows what incited Papa to hurl a priceless folio at the head of a loyal workman, who, most fortunately, was agile enough to duck, so that the book only drove out one panel of the studio door. We watch Papa throw chairs against the walls, bend cutlery between his teeth and beat his head with his fists in efforts to divert his inner typhoons. As a child I heard a choir sing 'Gladly the cross I bear' and thought the words were 'Daddy the cross-eyed bear'. May and I remember the time he threatened to send Mother's brand new piano out of the window because it arrived at dinner time. He doesn't like music much anyway, unless he has written it, and hates the sound of anyone practising piano: we are not allowed to begin until he leaves the house. Oxford friends nicknamed him Topsy, because his uncontrollable hair brought to mind the slave girl in Uncle Tom's Cabin who claimed to have grown and grown without any planning, as Papa's enthusiasms and furies seem to do.

To Mother he is 'Top'. 'Whatever he takes up,' she says, 'He is driven to excel. Top can't let go.' He worries and worries at it like a terrier shaking a rat. 'Unkind people gossip about your father's behaviour,' Mother told my sister and me when we were young, 'but we will refer to his tantrums only as naughtiness.' Embroidering Papa's designs was a notable talent of hers. 'He is a good man at heart, and a genius,' she says, 'and he loves us very much.' A genius at every art and craft except love. Even after Mother told Papa that she couldn't love him the way he wanted, still he wanted her. For too long he was sick with love for her. Imagine what people must have said when he brought his new bride Jane Burden into society: *A stablehand's*

daughter, snaring Morris, whose family are rich rich rich from copper mining! The largest copper and arsenic producer in the world, as it happens.

'Why did you marry my father when you felt such passion for Gabriel?' I demanded not long ago. The evidence is in every painting and drawing Gabriel did of her. At his bidding she was so often prone, awaiting him, her lips always pouting wetly, eyes brooding, brooding, bared neck arched, thrown back, a luscious split pomegranate clutched to her breast. Why did Papa concede to such flagrant public betrayal? Did he love some other woman, a forbidden one?

Mother told me that passion is a passing fancy, a flighty magic carpet you can't trust to stay aloft, whereas true love is a good rug laid down firm between four square walls, a safe place to bear children. 'Don't talk about Papa as if he were a horse blanket in a stable,' I shouted, and one of the conspirators gave me a strong dose of bromide.

A stable relationship? Truth is that you fall in love and then you fall to earth. If you're lucky, the magic carpet wasn't flying too high. Truth is the difference between a kept woman and a well-kept woman. Truth is that Gabriel Rossetti never asked for the burden of Mother's hand in marriage. *Asked for her hand.* As if you could separate it from the parts of her anatomy he wanted. He wrote her wonderful love letters, though, and she wrote back. When he and Mother were otherwise occupied I read his letters and wondered whether she could feel more passion for my father if he spoke to her, flirted with her the way Gabriel did. I overheard Wilfred Blunt and a friend of ours, *(they didn't notice me listening -*

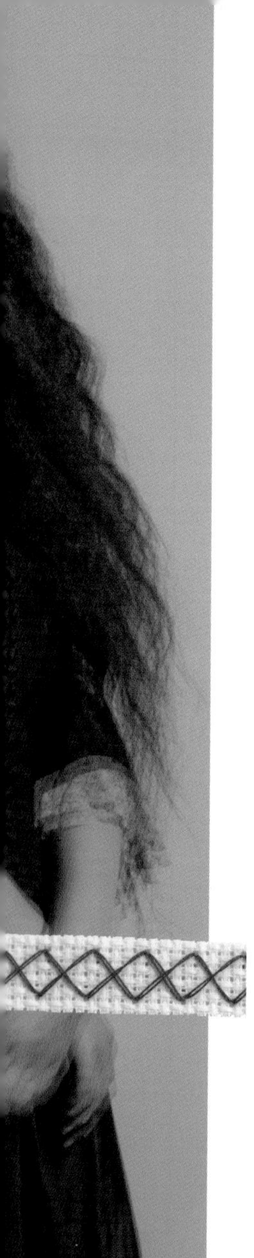

I am wallpaper to people outside my family): 'Morris is unique,' Blunt said, 'in that he has no thought for anything or person including himself, but only for his work and those who can help him with it. I have seen him act tenderly towards his eldest daughter Jenny and nice enough with her sister May and his wife, but I doubt whether he thinks of them much when he doesn't see them. His life isn't arranged with reference to them. The truth is that he will not give an hour of his time to anyone. He holds it to be too valuable.'

The truth, the truth. Truth is that Blunt has become Mother's second lover and it suits him to believe that Papa cares more for work than for us. Through Kelmscott Manor, our ancient country house, Mr. Blunt tip-toes. I 'hear' him in the way that I 'hear' epilepsy tip-toe through my brain. You see, the house is large and rambling, but few of its rooms are carpeted, their weary floors creak, every movement is heard from room to room, and where there are no movements one hears ghosts. The tapestried drawing room upstairs must be approached through Papa's bedchamber. Five tip-toe steps from his to Mother's. When Blunt visits Kelmscott he creaks the floorboards on his way to her (it wouldn't be Papa: for years he has slept alone). Deliberate creaks, I am certain: he enjoys the risk of being caught on his midnight prowls. Yet he is my father's friend and so was Gabriel, whose hot eyes melted my mother's defences while Papa dreamt of Icelandic maidens.

Does Mr. Blunt believe that I can't interpret his trespasser's creak? Perhaps. Like most people, he associates my condition with idiocy and swooning falls. They don't realise that in the days before fits my brain works faster, faster, fastest. I feel the urgent need to write, read, create. If only I were given paper and pen instead of bromide at those times, for I overflow with exhultation and revelations, which do not always lead to a hurricane mind. And *I* know when drugs are needed, I *recognise* the storms' approach. How can I explain the sensation to you? Imagine the way one senses an electric storm before it arrives - no, better still, imagine those nightmares where footsteps are creeping up behind as you walk alone down a tunnel late at night. A sense of wariness crawls over your skin, your whole body *listens* in expectation of danger approaching, time slows, the tunnel's end grows further away, you try to run, call for help but the law of nightmares prevents your flight. And then you wake.

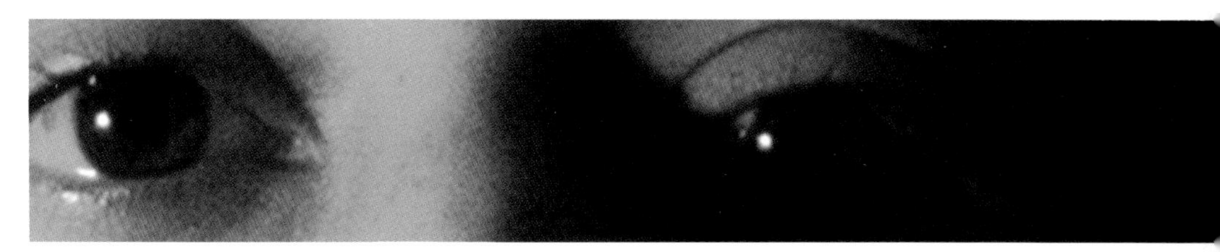

It is the same for me, except that I am constantly listening for those nightmare footsteps, even while awake, and when they do approach, 'real' sounds grow distant, I am overwhelmed by the murmurs of people I used to know, yet can't quite remember anymore. Their voices familiar but their words incomprehensible.

Physicians nod wisely and call this symptom, 'déja vu.' How wrong they are. Déja vu is a brief state, whereas mine lasts far longer. During it my consciousness doubles, as if I am standing outside myself. I am *over* conscious: aware that the sense of recurrance, however vivid, is but a morbid signal of the barbarian - the *Grand Mal* - about to seize and overthrow the castle of my mind. People with my condition can't escape the fear of those marauding footsteps, for one cannot escape one's *self*, can one? It is the randomness of seizures that crushes our souls. Regaining consciousness, we are exhausted, as if we have travelled a great distance without rest. We don't know how much time has passed, our speech is garbled, and although Language and Time do eventually return, some memories are wiped like chalk from a blackboard, leaving only dusty ghosts.

CHAPTER TWO

Doctor Q's Last Casebook *(1929)*

FIRST ENTRY

IS THIS LOCKED ROOM TO BE MY FINAL RESTING PLACE? Should it be so, then to whomever shall find my body I bequeath the following notes, and the unresolved mystery within them. To paraphrase Oscar Wilde, there are works one does not understand for a long time, one reason being that they bring answers to questions which have not yet been raised.

I will begin my strange love story at midnight in an attic corridor of Queen Square's Hospital for the Paralysed and Epileptic. Still in disrepair after the war, these corridors are rarely frequented, except by staff looking for yet more places to store old casenotes. A vast, uncatalogued archive we have here, so many fossils of past lives that one wag nicknamed our attic 'dead storage'. It includes relics from an era before the telephone, when even doctors' urgent exchanges regarding in-patients and out-patients were often conducted by letter or telegram. As a result of overcrowding from the war years, bookcases downstairs still remain half-hidden behind overflowing medical files and annual reports. Only last week a new secretary found a dusty copy of our 1918 Annual Report under the Boardroom's carpet.

I can almost hear my sweet Etta mocking that report, a self-satisfied piece of fiction in which our Governor had assured us that despite the Zeppelin raid of 1915, the hospital's reconstruction was proceeding 'slowly but surely'. (Very slowly, less than surely, Etta would have noted, viewing its still unreconstructed glory.) A bomb had scored a direct hit on Queen Square's lawn and substantially damaged our building, but - miracle of miracles - no one had been seriously hurt. 'A subject for sincere congratulations,' wrote the Governor (Of *whom?* asks my imaginary Etta), adding that, 'The transition to peace is chiefly a question of returning to their old work the members of our medical staff who were serving overseas.' Before long, he said, provision of hospital supplies, so difficult during the war, would become easier.

Easier? Eleven years later we remain understaffed, our finances strained by America's economic disaster, and another war looms, I feel certain, given the rise of that unhealthy political party in Germany. War begets war, just as epileptic seizures beget seizures, for some chamber of the human mind cherishes a battle. Do I sound unfeeling? In fact I feel too much, which is why I gave up active medical service in 1889.

Etta had also retreated from active service by then: in 1887 she had returned from the Bloody Sunday march on Trafalgar Square with her face so battered by a policeman's truncheon that it was almost unrecognisable. To protect the sensitivity of those in this hospital whose nerves were already damaged, she gave up nursing, the work she loved, learned shorthand (a skill my mentor William Gowers endorsed) and resigned herself to secretarial employment. 'Mustn't let this face of mine frighten the patients to death,' she'd said dryly. Very dryly.

Along this corridor is a long uninhabited room that I still think of as hers - so imagine my astonishment when its door opened at midnight and a woman emerged. Foolish of me to hope for a reincarnation, I know, and she looked to be in her late sixties, younger than Etta would be. Indeed, they bore no resemblance to each other: Etta was tiny and whippy as thread, my midnight visitor had a regal stature, unweighted by the almost medieval garnet necklace which graced her neck; a long ivory neck, a column, slightly corded by age. That her grey eyes, eerily luminous, were underlined by shadows only enhanced their power. For me, she epitomised the heavy-browed, antique beauty of the women one sees frescoed on Pompeii's tombs. A grave face, then.

An educated voice. 'Please help me, sir.' Beckoning me closer with one hand, she cradled in her arms, the way a mother cradles a baby, a bulky file resembling those we employ for casenotes. How had she come by it? No doctor would release his notes to a patient, and judging by her floorlength dress, she wasn't one of our nursing sisters, whose hemlines have been notably affected by the war, working briskly up from ankle to mid-calf.

'Are you lost, Madam?' I asked.

'No. I am looking for someone who worked at the old hospital. I mean the one torn down in 1882 and replaced by this one. I am told that you are

the last surviving doctor of that generation.'

I was mystified. 'Dilapidated though this corridor may be, Madam, it is a curious place to begin your search. A curious time of night, as well.'

'I would have approached you elsewhere, and earlier, but the staff explained that you have no consulting room here. They wouldn't give me your private address, understandably, but a nurse told me that you often haunted these corridors at night.'

'*Haunted?* Well, I have been retired from service for several years. Perhaps that is what she meant.'

Still holding her file tightly in one arm, she touched my hand. 'Please, sir, if you will spare me a few minutes, I can explain. The room behind us is comfortable enough.'

Not for me. Entering it, I was deafened by its former residents. *Dead storage.* Towers of dusty casebooks, medical charts and yellowed photographs battled for space. What was once a consulting room even smaller than the one Gowers used, had become, in effect, a dusty Freudian cupboard, medicine a neighbour to fiction and superstition, the desk overpopulated with primitive wood and ivory figurines who scrutinized bookshelves where neurological texts pressed closely against volumes by such epileptic authors as Dostoevsky, Flaubert, Tennyson, Edgar Allan Poe, Lewis Carroll. Opposite the bookshelves was a couch upholstered in a William Morris design rooted in the Middle-Eastern ornamentations that he and Freud admired. And, unheard of for a medical consulting room, the space is wallpapered, in a complex, overlarge design which, if not Morris's own, was clearly influenced by him.

Although I had not summoned the courage to set foot in that oppressive room in forty years, I had felt its magnetic pull each time I entered our hospital, for my beloved Etta had died on that very couch. August, 1889.

But let me return to how I came to be imprisoned.

The woman closed the door and moved to the left of the desk, leaving me little choice but to squeeze behind the couch. Her pale oval face, rising above the battalion of figurines, appeared disembodied, an uncanny effect enhanced by the flickering light. 'Welcome, Doctor, to the borderland of my unquiet mind,' she said, 'caught between sickness and sanity, between pit and pendulum. My home was one of the houses torn down in 1882 to build this hospital.' She began rocking her file and crooning a neurotic lullaby, 'Truth has few friends, lies have allies, all lies, all eyes. I am, Amen, I am, amended, I am, untended. But the conspirators might track me down even here. Walls have ears... Hear hear! Hearsay... Walls have voices, in one ear and out the other...' The lullaby wound down, and she placed her file on the desk next to a large pair of dressmaker's scissors.

EPILEPSY
CONDITIONS AFTER ATTACKS
CONDITIONS AFTER ATTACKS.
EPILEPSY
AND OTHER
CHRONIC CONVULSIVE DISEASES:
W. R. GOWERS M.D., F.R.C.P.
J. & A. CHURCHILL, NEW BURLINGTON STREET
1881
forgetful, sometimes irritable, and sometimes half
idiotic. The effect is often ascribed to the remedy used
The mental state of

'For my Pre-Raphaelite, Post-seizure dress,' she said, with a smile that would not have entirely reassured anyone in the medical profession who, like me, specialises in the diagnosis of neurological issues. Indeed, colleagues might suggest that I should have made the promptest of exits and located a stout orderly to escort her to a secure ward. Resurrect Hughlings Jackson (the neurological world's greatest seer, in my opinion), and he might advise that I was infected by madness the way epileptic brain cells are a 'mad part' of our brain that makes adjunct 'sane cells' act madly. But in my lifetime I have frequently served as an expert witness in the High Courts when it was essential to establish the difference between chronically dangerous psychotics and psycho-neurotics. Living by the precept that a physician should know diseases not only as a zoologist knows species, but as a hunter knows tigers, I felt confident that this woman posed no threat. However, my experience didn't protect me from a sense of unease. Not fear, understand, but claustrophobia, symptomatic of the mental condition I suffer.

'Might we open the door?' I asked. 'It is quite airless.'

'I need to speak to you alone.'

'We are unlikely to be disturbed up here, Madam.'

'You don't know the conspirators as I do. In the past they have had me followed and taken back.'

Taken back *where?* I wanted to ask, but the hot, close air was making me feel quite faint. The room seemed to rustle and bustle with lives other than our own, and its papered walls stirred, shifted and released the smell of damp vegetation. Up through Morris's design pushed an orchard of blood vessel trees, where pomegranates were transformed into coronal sections, wild tulips into temporal lobes. Rooted by arteries and branched with nerves, the cerebral grove began sprouting an undergrowth of those plants we employ to ease neurological disorders: mugwort and cannabis, valerian and belladonna. Belladonna, the Deadly Nightshade, confronted me. *You are hallucinating,* I told myself. Another symptom of my illness. I took deep breaths and tried to concentrate on the woman. Did she expect me to serve as weeder, wood-cutter, pruner of her disorderly mind? She had begun the lullaby again and her breathing grew ever more ragged, her language convulsed into hybrid nonsense, until, in one of those swings from mania to silence that epitomises her affliction, she ceased speaking altogether and for several minutes gazed silent into space. During that period I opened the door a fraction. When her eyes regained focus she said, 'Where were we, Doctor?'

My opinion was that she had suffered an 'absence' seizure, a malfunction of the brain which renders the epileptic temporarily blind, mute and deaf. To what distant land does the afflicted mind absent itself? Feeling that such a question, in these circumstances, was best kept to myself, I said that she had been about to tell me her name.

'My name?' She touched a pair of photographs on the wall. 'There I am. October 1879, aged eighteen.'

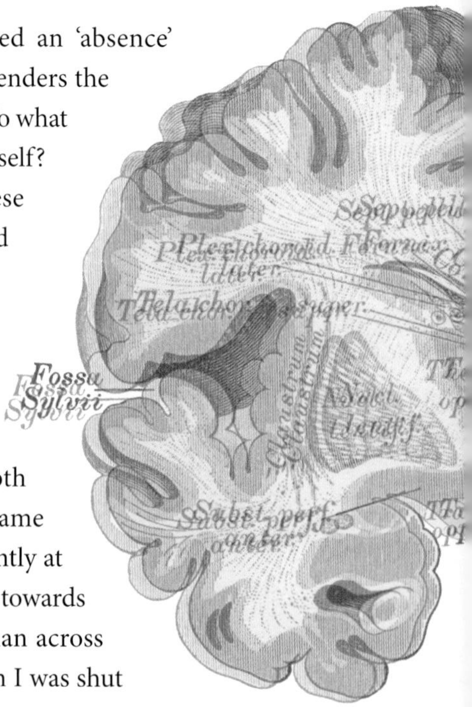

The two pictures resembled those taken of prison and asylum inmates. Both portrayed a young woman seated in the same position, except that in one she stared vacantly at the camera and in the other her head turned towards the left, expression unchanged. If the woman across the desk from me was telling the truth, then I was shut in with her father's tragedy, his guilty conscience - and my own.

CHAPTER THREE

2nd Recording: *Jenny Climbs*

(Pertaining to childhood years)

WE ARE JENNYANDMAY. Horrible Morris is the nickname we've given a cousin from our father's side. We never visit Mother's stable side, the Burdens, who live in Oxford. 'Her family is common as muck,' he taunts. 'She is a social climber.' What's wrong with climbing? We are good at it. Anyway, Mother's common sense is useful to profligate Papa, according to Aunt Bessie, her sister, who lives with us: 'Janey could shave shillings out of cowpats for him.' Why has Papa dubbed Aunt Bessie *Our boring Burden?*

Horrible Morris calls us 'Medieval brutes! Stable girls!'because the clothes Mother sews us have no hoops. But climbing is easier without hoops, and at Grandmamma's house beside Epping Forest we scramble up Papa's beloved hornbeams to pelt H.M. with insults. He declares women should wear bustles, so we shout that bustles make women look like bolsters tied in the middle or like fat goldfish with bustling tails swish swish behind. As protection against Horrible Morris we decided to buy swords and perhaps a gun, but had to settle for canes, as Mother didn't want us to hurt ourselves. She didn't mention H.M. or *his* health.

Epping is the Forestland where our father grew up, his wood beyond the world. With him we explored up and down from Wanstead to the Theydons and from Warren Hill to the Fairlop Oak, and read *Gerrard's Herball* cover to cover and can name every wild flower and native bird. We've watched adders resting languorous in the sun to warm their cold old blood, and discovered the site of Dr. Matthew Allen's lunatic asylum. Lord Tennyson, whom Papa admires, had interned himself there voluntarily while suffering from poetic bouts of nerves (and maybe epilepsy, but no one is sure about that). 'Do epilepsy and nerves make men poetic?' we asked Mother. Not necessarily, she said.

Kelmscott Manor is the flat Riverland, where Mother's family worked the soil not far away. They lie in it too. Among the wild tulips which run riot over the garden we sense the Burdens under our feet. Papa declares those tulips the beautifulest flowers on earth and recites *Hidden by tulips to his knee, his heart's desire his eyes did see.* His wallpaper designs give the tulips an orderly pattern, but 'You can't make desire orderly,' says Gabriel.

JennyandMay riot through the Manor's garretts and hide secrets between the floorboards. Occasionally we are separated by people's definition of us: Jenny the Clever Sister, mad about books, and May the Pretty Sister, good at Art. May is also good at escaping the Governess's Relentless Roman Ruins across Kelmscott's high roofs. Roof-riding, she watches our stream sliding and sucking dreamily into the distance. Once she got stuck in a saddle of the Manor's highest ridge and Mother said, 'You're old enough to know better.' Old Philip the gardener had to fetch the village's longest ladder. 'May should be sent to bed without supper,' the Governess said, but Mother was certain that May had learnt her lesson: 'Not to climb roofs.'

'Not to get stuck next time,' JennyandMay snapped in unison.

Mother's laugh came out as a quiet chuckle. She does everything quietly, especially around guests and Papa's family. JennyandMay heard Cook whisper to the maid, 'High up the social ladder as our Mrs. Morris has climbed, she hasn't dragged up her Oxfordshire accent far enough from the stable.'

'When we're old enough we're going to climb where no ladders can reach us,' we told Mother.

She is down to earth, feet on the ground. 'No such place, my loves.'

Jenny was born in the Red House, a green place, and May a year later, but JennyandMay began (age four and three) in Queen Square, rectangular on maps, though Mother describes it as a sooty circle where it's difficult to hide secrets. Everyone who is Anyone comes to admire Papa's upright genius and her reclining beauty. 'Warp and weft,' says Aunt Bessie, an embroiderer.

We live above Papa's Firm, surrounded by hospitals and charities for the nervous, the paralysed, the epileptic, the blind and other sorts of unhealthiness. But the School of Ecclesiastical Embroidery is here too, and

various institutions devoted to women's education, including the Female School of Art and the Working Women's College at Number 29 (to which Papa has kindly donated a few drawings). When JennyandMay asked Aunt Bessie why she kept slipping round there to attend an evening class (in Latin, of all things), she flustered as if accused of theft. 'I have no perspirations above my station!' she said. 'It's just... I'm for educatin' myself so as not to shame your Ma. I want to understand those Latin words I stitch for ecclesiastical folk.' Her chin came up. 'And I've made a friend at the college.' We'd seen the friend, a tiny woman with a face white as a doll's. Despite her size, she was strong enough to walk all the way from Islington and back every night to improve her learning, Aunt Bessie said. 'She calls herself "Made Marian", for she's no maid but has made good without help from men.' From her bag Aunt Bessie pulled a list. 'Marian's not like those grand folk round your Pa. Still, she knows their names and ways better than I do.'

'But most of these people are our close friends, Auntie! Partners in Papa's firm! They come here to dine every weekend - and you come round with us to the Faulkners at Number 35 regularly for tea.'

'Well my silly head can't seem to hold details of whether to Mister-Missus them or tell them to behave themselves, like I can do with Gabriel.'

We questioned how Made Marian knew about Papa's circle and Aunt Bessie tapped her nose, 'For me to know and you to find out.'

MARIAN'S LIST

MORRIS, MARSHALL, FAULKNER & CO, 'The Firm' (a 'Brotherhood' of seven old chums who fancy themselves Artists and Craftsmen, not Tradesmen), with their Consorts:

GABRIEL ROSSETTI, painter, poet, Pre-Raphaelite, partial to your sister Jane, but mind his straying hands, and don't mention his wife Lizzie: his Wicked Ways drove her to an early grave. CHARLEY FAULKNER, Confirmed Bachelor, though I've not myself confirmed his Dirty Deeds, part-time artist, good with numbers. (His Spinster Sisters KATE - jolly with Morris kiddies - and LUCY are dab hands with paints for The Firm.) EDWARD - Ned - BURNE-JONES, painter, Will Morris's friend and partner on books and buildings. (Wife GEORGIANA - Georgie - used to paint The Firm's tiles, among other Arty things, before Motherhood swallowed her whole. Kiddies: your nieces' chums MARGARET and PHILIP: don't muddle him with earlier Philip, who died). PHILIP WEBB, Architect, the Red House, Designer, Bachelor, a bit soft on Jane.

We didn't get through all the Brothers because on reading Mr. Webb's name May cried: 'Jam! He gives us blissful jam, jam and more jam. And tells us jokes we don't understand, but we laugh anyway, and he laughs too, and takes Mother to the opera because Papa won't. Jenny embroidered him a kettle-holder that he said was nicely worked, though it wasn't.'

'It was.'

'Wasn't.'

JennyandMay settled their differences by climbing to their bedroom and spreading their wings like birds in Papa's wallpaper designs. We stuck our tongues out at the men strolling across the square, the men who won't allow women, with or without bustles, to join their guilds. 'Ladies started the hospital, ladies keep the charities running,' says Aunt Bessie, 'and ladies like me and your Ma help embroider your father's tapestry tales, but who rules the roost? The cock-a-doodle-doos.'

'When we're old enough,' JennyandMay answer, 'we are going to form a guild for women where men are not allowed to join except in subordinate roles.' Grandmamma worries we'll never find husbands if we have that attitude, however loudly determined we are. Very loud. 'You're too old to make such a fearful racket, JennyandMay. You'll disturb your father's poetry.' Having finished his Earthly Paradise where none grow old, he is working on another Masterpiece set in medieval times. 'Weevil times,' Aunt Bessie teases him. 'Me and Janey have seen too many of them.' He's started reciting the verses to Mother but her Bad Backs come on quite quickly and she retires to bed or to Gabriel's studio in Chelsea, the way she did during the Paradise years while Papa read his epic stanzas aloud every night to friends in our living room. 'So far your Paradise is nigh on 40,000 lines,' Mr. Burne-Jones declared. 'I won't survive much more.' Mrs. B-J dug her fingernail into his hand whenever he dozed off. She used a pin on her own hand but her eyelids closed too, even though Papa always counts on her to stay awake. One night JennyandMay crept down from their bedroom to hear Papa recite the poem where the King has come to claim his bride and consummate his earthly quest, but is stopped by a hideous serpent coiling between him and his bride:

A huge dull-gleaming dreadful coil that rolled
In changing circles on the pavement fair.

LAT.
VENT.
LAT.
VENT.
CAUDATE
N.
INT.
CAPS.
INT.
CAPS.
INSULA
CLAUSTRUM
INSULA
CLAUSTRUM
III
V
CHIASMA
OT
ON
TEMP. LOBE
Mid. C.
Ant. Cerebral
Mid. C.
Int. Car.
Int. Car.
Reduce to 4 inches wide
HILL WOOD
Site of
Fairmead Lodge
EPPING NEW ROAD
FAIRMEAD BOTTOM
ROUND
THICKET
ALMSHOUSE
PLAIN
LONG HILLS
GREEN RIDE
PLAIN
PEAR TREE
PLAIN
Cuckoo
Pits
Gramston's
Oak
Cuckoo Brook
BUTTONSEED
CORNER
MAGPIE
HILL

Jenny felt the lines slither slide inside her, separating her from May, who whispered, 'Why did the bride blame the King for letting a serpent take her twixt the coils with sudden horror most unspeakable?'

'Shhhh.' Jenny didn't want her inside slithery feeling to end.

In the sing-song voice Papa used for poetry he evoked the bride's protest to her King: *They coil about me now, my lips to kiss, O love, why has thou brought me unto this?* Then the Governess discovered JennyandMay and dragged them away. 'You aren't old enough to hear such sauciness.' Old enough to know better, not old enough. No wonder Papa encourages us to celebrate the Middle Ages. 'A time when art and craft were appreciated more than speed and money!' he says. A time of swords and Crusaders, we thought.

That was in our minds when we initiated a Secret Society with our chums Margaret and Philip Burne-Jones. May was Honourable Secretary, Jenny was Captain, Margaret was Standard Bearer, Philip the Leader. *[Why should he be? Jenny complained to May. He is shorter than me and younger, and you can climb higher.]* At the first meeting a fire blazed in honour of each member and especially the Leader. For some reason Jenny was almost immediately charged with a crime, to await her trial and sentence at the next, which began with the Leader handing over a bottle of secret ink to the Secretary. Incense was burnt. At the trial Jenny was found guilty and sentenced to be degraded to Standard Bearer, receive twelve lashes and fifteen minutes in the darkest cupboard. Both were duly carried out. During the imprisonment, which lasted far longer than had been specified, the new Captain came to the door and whispered, 'Shall we mutiny against the Leader?' On her release Jenny told the Leader what had passed. To her great surprise (for she would never have thought a Leader could stoop so low) he laughed and told her it was a trick to test her loyalty. 'I instructed the Captain to say those words,' he said.

Jenny was hurt by Captain May's betrayal, and believed that it was wrong for her to have obeyed his instructions.

Not the last time my sister has betrayed me, Doctor.

CHAPTER FOUR

Doctor Q: *Second entry*

'I AM WILLIAM MORRIS'S ELDEST DAUGHTER,' she said. 'Jenny Morris, the epileptic.'

I found it hard to credit that this stately woman, her features still bearing traces of one who, in youth, had possessed great beauty, should be related to the vacant-eyed eighteen-year-old in the doubled photograph. Perhaps my scepticism was evident, for 'Jenny Morris' clenched her hands into fists, holding them up at me the way a pugilist would. Lowered again, unclenched, her fingers left half-moons of blood on the palms. '*Lunar* blood you judge it?' she said. 'A moony *loony's* blood?'

Our situation requiring a gentle approach, I tried to ignore the room's oppressive atmosphere and the memories it forced on me. 'You are here because of your condition, Madam?'

'I am here seeking evidence.'

'Evidence?'

'Of a conspiracy.'

I expected her to demand a reason for those photographs being on the hospital wall; instead she launched into an outpouring about how we should stick the label 'Spinning Jenny' on them. 'For I am subject to a multi-spindle machine around which the conspirators spin yarns to fit their own embroideries. They are unravelling my sense of time, space, matter, motion.' Grey eyes unfocussed now, full of cobwebs, she proceeded on a meandering route through facts tangled in irrelevant details and digressions, invented aphorisms, repetition. Such unrelenting prolixity is common enough to epileptics, particularly when a seizure is about to occur.

'Why do you stare at me like that, Doctor, as if I were squirming under a microscope?'

Her abrupt volte-face from nonsense back to sense was startling, and it took me a moment to respond. 'Forgive me, Madam. I am old, absent-minded.' *Absence-minded.* And unconvinced as yet by her claim to

Morris heritage. 'Please tell me how I may be of assistance.'

Almost accusatory, she stated: 'Uncover the truth about my father's relationship with your hospital.'

'Relationship? What relationship, Madam?

'There must have been one. Papa and his factory occupied Number 26 Queen Square for seventeen years. Right next door to you.'

Her blunt approach and the direction she was headed unnerved me. Struggling to decide which course of action would do her least damage, I played for time, assuring myself that truth should wait until she was less emotional, less confrontational. 'My employment here didn't begin until 1880, Madam. By which time our staff and the hospital had grown considerably.'

Her mouth tightened. '1865 to 1881 the Morris design firm operated from Queen Square. Papa's most celebrated poetic saga was composed here: *The Earthly Paradise* - all England read it. Members of your profession too, I believe.' She smiled. 'During the first seven years at Queen Square my family lived "above the shop", so to speak, and even after we moved to another house, Papa maintained a bedroom and studio here, and my mother continued to work for the firm. No one crossing this square could fail to recognise my mother.'

I could have gone further and stated that no one who knew William Morris failed to recognise the stamina of his wife, is beautiful, oft-painted wife. To live with him *and* an epileptic daughter? Jane must have felt - Jane did feel... But where could this conversation lead us except towards a place I didn't wish to go? The Firm, infirm. 'Your father was widely celebrated,' I began, 'Nevertheless -' Nevertheless, *what?*

Patiently she waited for me to continue, but I had stalled, searching for excuses, and so, relentless, my Prosecutor built her case. 'During the firm's last five years here I was suffering from epilepsy - and your hospital was the first dedicated entirely to curing the epileptic and paralysed. Its staff members walked past our door every day, Papa shared the odd game of bowls with them, he frequented a pub on this square, there were female medical students who studied at the Working Women's College, which he helped to decorate. Even this building - opened four years after Papa left - bears his influence.'

Not surprisingly. Years ago, Etta had stitched me a map that spanned the Morris years, with Queen Square as a focal point - a Pantheon where art and science intersected, interacted. It was an era when map-makers in the labyrinthine human brain strode these corridors and still found time to draw, etch, paint; when eminent physicians rubbed shoulders with craftsmen and craftswomen at lectures given by John Ruskin. Why, Gowers once stopped a carriage just to get out and shake hands with Ruskin, whom he admired enormously, but had never met. Imagine a physician today saying, as Gowers did, that the proudest moment of his life was having his etching exhibited by the Royal Academy. A Golden Age. While other explorers were building empires in lands most of us will never see, we neurologists were mapping the brain's wrinkled geography, and, though shared by all humans, it remains virtually *terra incognita*.

I still have Etta's map. Most prominent on it are the institutions dedicated to uniting and educating women who wished to escape dependence on men. Thanks to those institutions Etta had worked her way up from servant to seamstress to nurse. 'A stitchy witch', she had been dubbed by Victor Horsley (most notable of our brain surgeons), 'charged with mending broken spirits.' Their admiration was mutual: she greatly appreciated young Horsley's support for women's suffrage, her only complaint being that he also supported teetotalism.

These fond memories were no help in coping with Jenny Morris (for it *was* she, I had accepted), who summed up with a shrug, 'In short, you must have known my father.'

'Knew *of* him, of course,' I blustered. 'Who could not? But the members of my profession with whom he familiarised didn't occupy minor posts, as I did then. In 1880 I was twenty-two and your father -'

'Forty-six.'

'I worked impossibly long hours, with any "spare" time devoted to research. Indeed, my first two years were spent writing papers. As for poetry...'

God, what determination one would need to survive Morris's volcanoes of sexual anxiety. His unearthly Paradise, a Nordic vision of Chaucer's Canterbury Tales, is inhabited by swooners who prophesy even as they swoon. Knights fall to the earth in ecstasy and thrash their limbs, blood gushing from their mouths, at the entrance to engulfing caverns where entrancing females lurk, ready to betray. The Vesuvian outpouring from Morris makes me sympathise with readers of my academic papers who complain that these are more like first drafts which, instead of pruning, I have allowed to sprout thickets of amendments, parentheses and afterthoughts, supported by roots of lengthy footnotes.

'As for poetry?' said Jenny, smiling as if the subject could or would draw us together. Her expectation of greater intimacy made me uncomfortable.

Why did I stay, then? Those who believe in an Afterlife might claim that it was Etta's generous spirit - pressing me, as she had many times, to give my patients a voice: 'Learn the vocabulary and grammar of their silences,' she would say, her advice echoing Gowers. He never lost sight of our patients' emotional needs. 'Enter into their feelings,' he urged us all, 'and thus ensure a tenderness in dealing with them.'

With this in mind, I apologised to Jenny and confessed that my literary taste leaned away from poetry towards Wilkie Collins, Conan Doyle, writers of their ilk. 'In my youth I sank so low as the "penny dreadfuls", Miss Morris,' A taste I kept secret from Professor Maudsley, 'Father of British Psychiatry', who asserted to the neurological world that the modern sensation novel, with its murders and bigamies, was an achievement of the 'epileptic' imagination, 'apt to occupy itself with painful or repulsive subjects'.

His theory had amused Etta. I remember her, comfortably naked after the first time we made love, reading from a gothic mystery. She began in the middle. 'Stop,' I protested. 'This book is unfamiliar to me. Give me its plot, its setting, its characters.'

'Just the usual,' she said, her eyes teasing. 'A dark and stormy night. An unnamed narrator: murderer or bigamist? Stories buried within stories within a mysterious manuscript. Sexual transgressions, sinister portraits, Doppelgangers, vampires, unscrupulous doctors, and -' She flicked through pages. 'And the obligatory sane victim locked away in an asylum.'

'A *heady* brew,' I said, and was gratified by her chuckle. 'Vampire or victim?' she asked, rolling on top of me. 'Please diagnose.' Her literary synopses at bedtime became a joke between us. Foreplay, often as not.

'Your silences grow ever longer,' said Jenny Morris. 'Does it take so much consideration to admit that you have never read my father's work?'

'Alas, the closest I get to poetic is the work of Robert Louis Stevenson. A great supporter of our hospital, by the way.'

'Stevenson, presumably, found no Jekyll or Hyde within these walls.'

'I trust not.' What he found was the setting for his tale, as well as advice from my teacher Russell Reynolds on the duality caused by psychoneurotic illnesses. At the time, society was rife with fears about physicians who meddled in the brain, fears encouraged by journalists hoping to earn a few extra shillings from their editors. Even the drama folk profited, for in September 1888, the very month that a theatre version of Jekyll and Hyde arrived on London's stage, Jack the Ripper stalked through Whitechapel. Our esteemed Reynolds, who had received free tickets to the play, dismissed it and pronounced, 'I paid too much.' Reynolds always had close associations with the creative world. An accomplished painter himself, it was he who introduced me (then a student) to William Morris in 1877. 'Fascinating specimen,' Reynolds said before we arrived. 'Note the chaos of his studio, manic with verse and dyes. I've known him to take up a dozen projects at once and then lose interest in them, but his obsession with indigo dye is almost religious.' On another visit we made the mistake of interrupting the great designer's experiments in blue, and he bellowed (not entirely good-humouredly): 'Are you blind? I am dyeing! I am dyeing!'

You must have grasped by now that Morris's was an era when this hospital had already achieved world fame, justifiable fame. How is it then that during the thirty-three years since his death one discovers in no Morris biography, no Morris eulogy or letter, any mention of this establishment, except *en passant*? No suggestions of any relationship between Morris and us, no hint at the implications of our proximity. His secret has been successfully kept secret. About this secrecy I am ambivalent - a dangerous ambivalence, it transpires, for the result is that I have been, I remain, always close to dying.

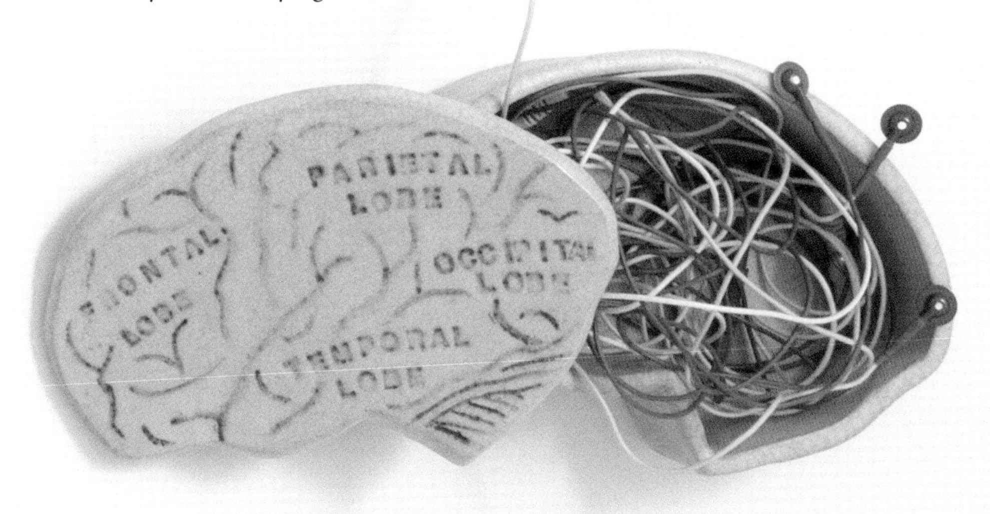

CHAPTER FIVE

3rd Recording: *Jenny Dyes*

(Pertaining to the years 1872 - 1876)

MY FATHER IS A COLOURFUL CHARACTER, people say. Inside our house the air is saturated with his colour. Hating chemical dyes because they are too bright and lack a sense of history, he has become a sorcerer with walnut roots and husks and poplar twigs, and studied the kermes insect's habits so that he can produce the vermilion used in medieval times. When he gets wrought up by a colour's refusal (or a dyer's or a workman's) to meet his elevated standards, Mother whispers, *Double, double, toil and trouble*, her private code that warns him not to let his cauldron nature bubble over. At supper one night with Gabriel, Papa was discussing Kelmscott Manor, which they began leasing in 1871. The painting studio is hung with old tapestries portraying Samson and Delilah, and Papa declared that although the tapestries were never great works of art, they look better now than they did originally. 'The yellow dye, being fugitive, has faded and left the greens nearer to indigo.' The colour nearest to his heart.

'Come now, Topsy,' said Gabriel. 'Why keep a thing when its colours are no longer true?'

Papa asserted that the tapestries give an air of romance, 'and make the walls a pleasant background for the living people who haunt the room.'

'Nonsense. Those faded cloths portray Samson betrayed by a wicked temptress, then blinded and fettered. Only *you* would find the tale romantic.' Papa's expression changed from dreamy to ragged, which made me feel guilty, having upset him earlier by stating that brains are ugly, not like the hand-coloured engravings in anatomy books. My knowledge came from having secretly ventured into the hospital next door, and there I had snatched a look at a dead brain. 'The colour of an overcooked cauliflower,' I told Papa.

May and I were taught by him to appreciate that colour alters perceptions. Moving to Queen Square, he had transformed the ballroom into workshops, and in one long wooden corridor connected to our house sat the stained glass painters, whom May and I loved to watch. Their corridor overlooked the flowerboxes where we decided to bury Lady Audley. Yellow-haired Lady Audley, May's favourite doll, was named after the blonde governess in a magazine we read. On her gravestone we felt obliged to write that her namesake deserted her child and killed various men by drowning and fire. The burial ceremony made the glass painters laugh so loudly that Papa forbade us to trespass on their territory again. 'You disturb them,' he said. Aunt Bessie suggested to Mother that however much he respects working class people, he prefers them working at a respectable distance.

My sister and me he called 'the Littles', but trusted us with our own dye kits of queer lumps and powders. Stencilling peacock tints onto wallpaper, I pitied the clients who come to visit the Firm's showrooms, because the fabrics are displayed on white walls, whereas the room my sister and I share is papered with 'Trellis', which I love. It frightens May. 'The birds are too alive,' she told Gabriel after the argument about faded colours. 'The trellis looks like a cage.' He clearly found her comment amusing, but Papa turned

vermilion with temper, which amused Gabriel even more. 'Dangerous stuff, your wallpaper,' he said. 'Met a doctor at the Royal Academy - Russell Reynolds by name, friend of my own quack. He has treated decorators who developed convulsions from hanging rolls of Scheele's Green wallpaper.' Gabriel's black eyes sparkled like jet beads, and he quoted Papa's maxim:

Whatever you have in your rooms think first of the walls, for they are that which makes your house and home. 'Have I got that right, Topsy?' Gabriel inquired of his pet wombat, whom he had set on a chair as if it were a guest.

Already in a bad mood, Papa wrapped his legs around his chair and squeezed them in the jerky way he has which is hard on insubstantial furnishings. The chair creaked in protest and I creaked too, knowing he dislikes that wombat (although it is stuffed, having died some years earlier), perhaps because of the cartoon Gabriel did of it on a leash held by Mother. Tension built and pressed against my head. 'Why would green be poisonous?' I asked, familiar with many ways people can poison each other.

'The arsenic employed to make the colour escapes into the air,' answered Gabriel. Mother glared at him and whispered *Double, double* to Papa, but Papa's expression indicated that the cauldron bubbled ever faster. 'Damp climates,' Gabriel carried on, 'encourage a fungal growth in the wallpaper and make the poison volatile. Gives off an odour of garlic - or mouse droppings, depending on who you ask.'

May, eyes darting between us, also felt the bubbling tension. 'Mouse doesn't smell,' she piped up. 'You remember Mouse, don't you Gabriel?

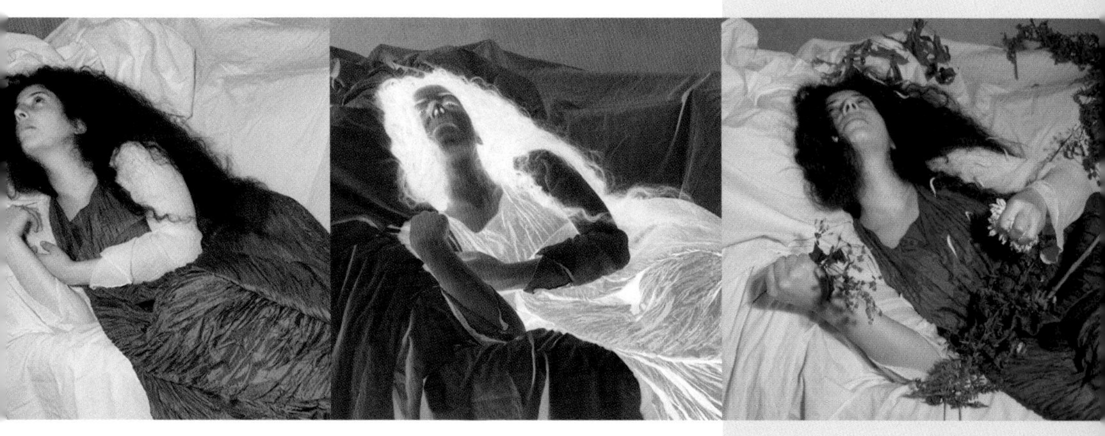

The pony Papa brought back from Iceland last summer when you were staying with Mother and Jenny and me at Kelmscott.'

'How could I forget those two sultry months? Your father exploring glaciers and straddling Icelandic ponies while I assumed his position in the Manor.' He stroked May's cheek. 'Ensure Mouse doesn't lick any green wallpaper, my sweet. Reynolds told me it can cause seizures, memory loss, psychosis, *impotence* -'

'Folly folly folly!' Papa leapt to his feet. There was a loud crack from the chair. One of its legs had broken off. He picked up Gabriel's wombat and hurled it across the room. 'This arsenic wallpaper scare - a greater folly is impossible to imagine! Doctors have been bitten as people are bitten by witch fever! Licking wallpaper? Who would do such a thing!'

'No one would, Papa,' I soothed him. 'Even Mouse.'

I didn't begin licking wallpaper until this year. 1876, a date embedded in me like an ammonite in stone. Three years ago Papa moved us to the house Mother describes as a very good size for one person to live in, or perhaps two. Obviously not big enough for Aunt Bessie as well, so we had to leave her behind, though she stays with us when Papa isn't home. Having become even more passionate about colour, he often sleeps at Queen Square, where he has converted the larder into a temporary dye-house. He spends more and more time in the northern town of Leek. Although it is famous for manufacturing the aniline dyes he hates, he has found in it a kindred spirit - Thomas Wardle, an expert on dyestuffs who is helping him experiment with medieval recipes for colour. Up and down, up and down to Leek Papa travels. Up and down like a bride's nightie, says Aunt Bessie. Friends nickname him Blue Topsy because his hands are stained blue from perpetually dipping them into indigo vats.

'Instead of into you,' Gabriel said to Mother, who snapped, 'Hold your noise!'

Gabriel doesn't, though, which I suspect is the reason Papa evicted him from Kelmscott two years ago and took over its lease. May and I can see how unhappy our parents are. We try, each in our own way, to ease Papa's spirits. 'Because he is least to blame,' says May. She thinks he will be consoled by her acting as his devoted shadow, quietly pinpricking and pouncing his designs - too quietly, I fear. He doesn't appreciate that she is learning to interpret his ideas even before he has them. She aspires to be like Agnes Garrett, who has set up the first all-female interior decoration business, its designs inspired by Papa's. My model used to be the other Garrett sister: she became a doctor despite the male doctors' attempts to prevent her. Determined to make our father proud, I studied very hard, my heart set on becoming a scholar. Or perhaps a scholarly revolutionary!

'If Jenny wants a husband, she mustn't spend her life buried in books,' Gran warned Papa as he headed off for Leek again. Ha! Long ago I had realised that embroidery and marriage were not for me, that I would be happy to die, unwed, in a grave lined with books. I tried to impress this on every physician Mother consulted about the shaking fits I started having just before my Cambridge Local examinations. The first doctor who came to our house muttered and murmured at Papa: *Ahem... Girls of a certain age... Nerves, don't you know...*

'It isn't girlish fits of nerves she suffers from,' Mother said, quite loudly for someone famously silent.

The old quack drew himself up to his full height, just below her chin, and declared that competitive examinations were overstressful - even dangerous - for people with my condition. When I asked him to tell me the nature of my 'condition', he addressed Papa, as if Mother and I weren't there. 'Overstimulated, your daughter could smother in a pillow while she was unconscious, Mr. Morris.' (*And leave blood on the linen from biting her tongue*, whispered May. Only she and Aunt Bessie knew that I suffered nightly fits as well as daily, and both were sworn to secrecy.)

'Intellectual endeavours,' the doctor went on, 'overstimulate a young girl's brain, potentially leading to hysteria.'

The only medicine he could recommend for the headaches that precede my fits was a bitter extract of willow bark. After he left, we looked as if we'd swallowed a bottle each, so bitter were our expressions. Aunt Bessie later added to the willow bark a decoction of mugwort and valerian leaves. 'They might relieve your fits without you having to give up them books you loves, my pet.'

A parade of physicians, ever more eminent, marched through our house, until we were honoured by John Russell Reynolds. After Mother and Papa had recited my symptoms yet again, he embarked on a lengthy description of how they should be managed. 'To avoid *status epilepticus*,' he said, at which I interrupted in Latin, '*Primum non nocere*, Doctor: First

do no harm.' He complimented my scholarship, and then informed Papa that outdoor life was better for the epileptic than was a sedentary occupation.

'Couldn't one fall out of a tree one was climbing?' May asked, and Reynolds suggested that her sister avoid climbing. 'Jenny turns an ugly shade of blue when having a fit,' May responded, 'even if she's lying down.'

'Blue, you say?' He glanced at Papa, who nodded. 'That is cyanosis, Mr. Morris. Indication of the respiratory muscles being highly compressed.' Another prescription was duly prescribed, this one for potassium bromide. It makes me feel quite incapable of climbing anything, especially those intellectual heights once predicted for me. No one discusses them anymore, and we don't discuss how my illness will affect May's future. I am contagious, a choking weed, not a tulip, my seizures have disorderly patterns, my colours are no longer true. Will Papa continue to cherish me, like those old tapestries he loves, or roll me up, lock me away?

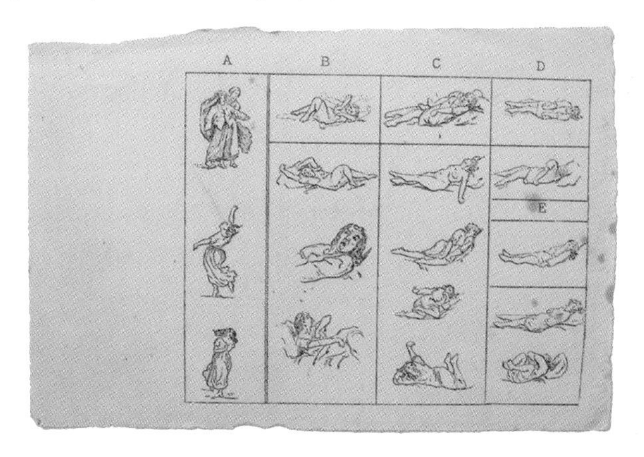

1876 1876 1876. Licking and then chewing Papa's Acanthus wallpaper as one does toffee apples, I am disappointed to find that the poison doesn't work. Still, Papa last year gave up directorship of the copperworks, where arsenic is mined. 'Rejected arsenic only because its profits were reclining,' Gabriel sneers to anyone who will listen, 'and subjected the Brotherhood to a poisonous year of negotiations in order to make our design firm his own.' But under Papa's directorship The Firm is thriving. Poisonous arsenic can be sublime, you understand: sublimated, the process whereby a solid is transformed into a spirit without passing through a liquid phase. Papa and I: our love solid, spirited, then sublimated. *By the pricking of my thumbs, something wicked this way comes.*

CHAPTER SIX

THE STOLEN MEMORIES of JANE MORRIS

A Letter (1876)

My dearest Gabriel

This is a most difficult letter to write, please forgive me in advance if it causes much distress. I can no longer sit to you in the future. The reason is not what you think, though I confess your gloominess in Bognor last winter did cast me down – more from the fact that clearly I can do nothing to help you from these glooms than any pain I felt for myself – though it does grieve me to see you so, as it has done since the dreadful days four years ago.

Now I have worse grief – Jenny's falls and fainting fits are discovered to be caused by epilepsy. Her convulsions are *grand mals*, if you know what that means. The doctors did not want to say so at first, but the last time was so serious that Top demanded an explanation.

Poor Jenny is devastated. She had just – this is very cruel – finished those exams she took to study at university and a fortnight ago heard that she had passed. Now she must give up all studying, and all hope too – they say brainwork overstretches the mind. I took her out of school at once – May too, and both girls are now with me in Kent. Most days pass quietly, but the worst is never knowing when a fit will happen again.

We must – I must – devote myself to caring and finding a cure for this terrible affliction. The doctors say there is no cure, but careful management can do much. They have prescribed a heap of remedies, quite useless I'm sure. But we have hope – many days pass without incident and even sometimes a week or more, so surely it may vanish as suddenly as it came?

Luckily we are no longer living at Queen Square, where it would be impossible to keep this from the knowledge of the Firm's workmen, who are so fond of Jenny and May. It is heart-breaking. We have told only a few friends – please keep this news to yourself: it will be dreadful for both girls if it gets about. The doctors, of course – those mad-doctors in Queen Square we used always to joke about – say it is 'a most interesting case', but to me it is a thunderbolt, a blow that has thrown us upside down. We will have to move from Turnham Green to a larger house with rooms for a nurse-companion. They say Jenny must never be left alone. She must always be calm, never upset or excited or angry. But she is all those.

So that is why. You will always be welcome, naturally, when we have a new home. Jenny and May will be pleased to see you – though I daresay you will not feel inclined. But I cannot come to sit – not in Chelsea nor anywhere you choose in the country.

Top blames himself. The doctors asked if any members of our families suffered. I thought of my father's drunken rages, then Top said Jenny's grandmother has long had sudden lapses, when she stops and stares. This they say may be a benign form of the disease. Top too has this: you know how we used to chaff and tease him till he lost his temper, you remember how we laughed. He would seem quite transported, then stop, shake his hair and as it were come back to us. So he blames himself. But that is not like Jenny's attacks. He never falls down.

Yet he has these... <u>explosions</u>; no one knows better than myself his sudden, unlooked for fury. You have occasionally seen it – his fist smashing the table, the violent burst of abuse. What neither you nor anyone else has ever known is how it has been turned against me. At first it frightened me: I had thought Top – and all you his friends too – were such gentlemen who were always gentle with women, unlike the brute who was my father. Then I learned that all men can be violent. You do not know that is why my marriage failed. I am blamed for coldness, cruelty, ingratitude to the great poet who condescended to take an ostler's ugly ignorant daughter to wife.

I am grateful indeed. And Top, when the hateful words, the blows even, are over – he is always contrite, ashamed. And he must be forgiven, for without him I have nothing, I am nothing. What can't be changed must be endured.

But I believe we shall find a cure for Jenny. At present the doctors prescribe only change of air, change of scene, tranquillity. So we are in Deal, the very dullest place to be found. The Howards have invited us to winter in Italy – this year or next, whenever is best for us, and I believe the climate there will do Jenny good: do you not think warm (not hot) sun and gentle breezes are healthful? At any rate it will do me good, and May too; we are all much confined indoors as a result of Jenny's affliction. May can join George Howard painting outdoors and Jenny play with the children, who do not understand her trouble. Of course, we shall rent a separate villa, but close by. It is a godsend and Rosalind an angel for thinking of us. If you see them, you may please tell them how grateful I am.

Dearest Gabriel – how terrible that I should visit Italy for the first time without you! We used to dream of it so – the travels we should make to the land of Dante and Cavalcanti! I learnt the language – your language, with your sister a stern yet patient teacher. How all is changed! She is gone, I am but a scarecrow, you hardly better. I could weep; indeed, I do weep, but silently, so Jenny will not overhear.

I always loved you. You wrote once that I did not believe in the strength of your love for me – but it is I who should claim that. I can no longer be part of your life but I will always love you.

Burn this letter. I have never written this before, and fear if not destroyed it will fall into unfriendly hands. But I want to write it at least once, caro mio. This is not farewell, but it is the end.

No, I cannot send this – it will grieve you too much. I do not want you to think again of the opiate-and-whisky. I will keep it in the box with all your letters, and hide them somewhere safe. One day perhaps when we are all dead they will be found and people will understand.

Scraps torn from Jane's undated pages

We stitched the coverlet together, Jenny and I. I hoped it would calm her, keep her brain quiet, the steady stem stitch, chain stitch, laying the silks on the pounced lines. Can you tell my stitches from hers? Sometimes she would stitch the stems, I the leaves. Then she would choose the leaves, or the big petals. The fritillaries were my favourites: they only grow at Kelmscott, not in London, however many plants we try to move. Their heads droop like bells, like Jenny's when she is most sad and silent.

Ten more minutes, then you must rest your eyes.

Looking at the quilt, you cannot guess an invalid had a hand in it. That is so mysterious to me: how at this moment she will be carefully drawing the needle through, or tightening the next stretch of linen, and then, the fever, the fit, whatever horrible thing it is, attacks. We see it coming and force her down, on the couch or on the floor, hold her down till it passes away. Each time it's a knife in my heart: I should know now nothing can be done, but if we go a whole day quietly, or three, five days, my hopes return. I can't stop them.

They say it is best to keep her quiet, calm, in a tranquil atmosphere. I used to like sitting silently, while Gabriel was drawing, or working away at the altar-cloths, curtains, embroidered cushions, collars, slippers. But now the silence frightens: I feel I am waiting for the next time the thing will seize dear Jenny, my Jenny. How can I keep it away, at bay?

Take the deep crimson and lay it against the silver-green. They seem to stroke each other. Though strong, the colours are restful.

If we could only get that restfulness into your brain.

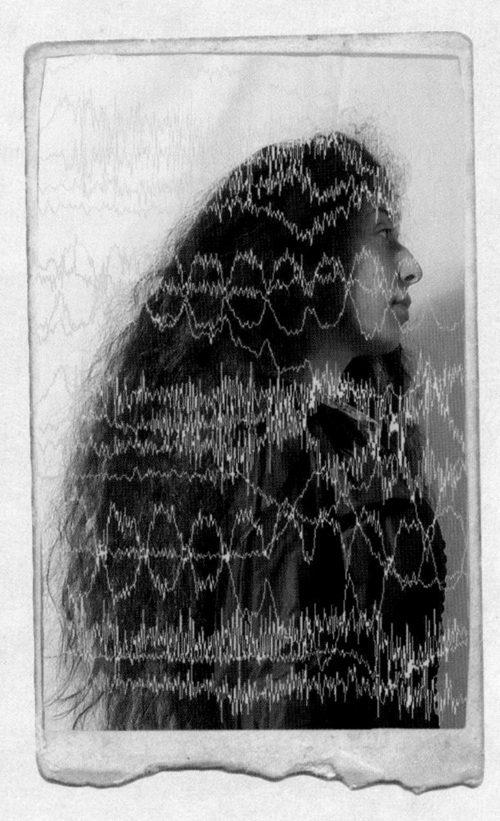

Georgie says sometimes it helps to write things down: otherwise they keep haunting you. She says I cannot undo things by silence.

Silence has served me well. If you don't speak, no one knows what you are thinking, or how ignorant you are. Or how anguished. In all the years since Jenny's first seizures I have wanted not to be pitied, most especially by those who grudged and grumbled at my good fortune. But the pain is unbearable. So bad that I have told Mr. Blunt some of it; and he will blab, being a gossip; mea culpa.

CHAPTER SEVEN

Doctor Q: *Third entry*

WATERY METAPHORS SUIT THE EPILEPTIC DREAMY STATE, I thought, watching Jenny drift towards what Edgar Allan Poe had termed 'the gulf beyond'. As absence engulfed her, I leaned over to touch a pillow on the couch, embroidered by Etta when she could no longer stand. Illness had stolen her voice by then, though to judge by her handwritten notes, her wit was unimpaired: *Let me shuttle off this mortal coil, my love.* When I stubbornly refused to untie our knot, she used a needle. 'To make a point,' she stitched; like Jane and May Morris, Etta's metaphors were textile, whether expressed through cloth or flesh.

HAVE NOTHING IN YOUR HOUSES
THAT YOU DO NOT KNOW TO BE USEFUL
OR BELIEVE TO BE BEAUTIFUL.

William Morris, 'The Beauty of Life' (1880)

'I was never beautiful,' said Jenny, drifting back again, 'and from 1876 onwards I was worse than useless. Still, Papa never exiled me for good. He decided that my wayward mother, whose role until then was to keep the books and the house and be beautiful and stitch prettily, should add home-nursing to her list of skills. Poor Mother, entwined between us. *Obliged* to be entwined.' Jenny picked up the scissors, opened and closed them three times. Keen-edged, they sheared the air like silk. 'Epilepsy and embroidery stitched cross-purposes through her life. She couldn't love me, I felt certain. She couldn't even enjoy embroidering with me because it left my mind free to concentrate on intellectual matters, which set my brain at war: the doctors were right and I hated them for their rightness. I sharpened my resentment on Mother, as if she were to blame.' Snip went the scissors. 'Aware that she couldn't cope with me on her own, Papa hired a nurse to assist her. A succession of them.' Snip, snip, snip. 'One proved so brutal she was dismissed.' Not soon enough, Jenny's scissors implied. 'It didn't take long before Papa agreed to alternate home-nursing with short periods at nursing homes. In these I could be "plausibly contained", as one doctor put it. I flew into rages, he said. Where else was there to fly?' Scissors close to her mouth now, she spoke in a monotone, as if to a recording machine.

Who would the blades snip next, I wondered, and found my eyes straying towards the door.

'May says that our parents were forever "beside themselves" because of me, Doctor. But brains are always beside themselves, I think. A marriage of two minds, right and left, and down the middle a great divide, bound by a fibre that conveys an intimate, ongoing dialogue.' She tilted her head side to side. 'My family: two hemispheres, two temporal lobes. A temporal love.' A tempered smile at me. 'So beside himself was Papa that one weekend in the first summer of my illness he managed to write only 250 lines of his poem "Sigurd the Volsung and the Fall of the Niblungs". Under less stressful circumstances he was capable of 750 lines per *night*.' She scissored the double photograph of herself in half, quarters, editing the implication of her statement. Then, laying her scissors down, she withdrew a letter from the file. 'Four months after I was diagnosed, Papa wrote this to my grandmother. I borrowed it from her.' That tilt of her head again. 'Stole it - and made a copy. Read the sentence I underlined.'

October 24, 1876

My new book will be out in about a month... I am somewhat dyspeptic, but it don't go for much. Jenny is now regularly at her boarding house, and calls herself a 'Poor Exile', though to say the truth she likes it very much: she had a tumble last Friday, a very slight one, that was the first for three weeks. She looks so well that I can't help thinking she must soon get over it all. May is rather poorly, she is not very strong and looks more of an invalid than Jenny...

'Bromide,' said Jenny. I thought she was judging the sentiments expressed by Morris, whose letter resonated with a desire to free himself of family sagas and return to the Vikings. In fact she was judging the drug,

described by someone she'd met as 'a chemical castrator' employed to quell the licentious behaviour common among soldiers. 'And epileptics,' Jenny said. 'Our natures incline towards licentiousness. Or so I've been told by the doctors who quelled my brain with bromide.' She let me consider that for a moment. 'Infinitely more frustrating to me is the way bromide castrates the mind. But I imagine that is what neurologists desire to achieve?'

Was I expected to defend my entire profession, including its most misguided practioners? All I could do was offer sympathy to Jenny for any bitter experiences she had suffered at their hands, and assure her that her frustration was perfectly understandable. 'However, Miss Morris -' *However, nevertheless, despite, notwithstanding:* our story is replete with qualifiers and disconnections, a disconnection syndrome which in my case has lead to dysfunction. 'However,' I pressed on, 'for neurological disorders bromide is the most reliable treatment.' By 1899 this hospital was dispensing near two tons of the stuff. When bromide failed, we had to rely on cocktails of arsenic, chloroform, opium, cocaine, cannabis, strychnine, chloral. Poor Rossetti: an addiction to chloral and Morris's wife had finished him off.

'Let me assure you, Miss Morris, that I have always been in agreement with the great William Gowers, who -'

'Gowers?'

'A physician at this hospital. He decried the idea of 'bromising', as did many of us. We wished to suppress our patients' fits, not their minds. And if I may say so, your mind doesn't seem over-bromised.' Her eyes had taken on the scissor blades' flashing metallic quality.

'Perhaps not tonight, sir. My latest nurse-companion accepts that I prefer to have more seizures rather than more bromide.' Retrieving her father's letter, she applied the scissors - snip snip and his page of self-delusion was confetti. 'Too often the drug has been forced on me, you understand. Still, all epileptics become accustomed to random seizures by hostile forces, inside our brains and out. My parents weren't hostile, they did their best, but I always wondered why the nursing establishments and boarding houses they sent me to were never close to London or Kelmscott Manor.'

'Alternative treatments -'

'That was one reason given. "Healthier air" another. Wasn't our green Kelmscott Manor healthy? Couldn't a nurse-companion have been installed there? Loving sick people, I conclude, must be easier at a distance. Sent away I was, brought home, sent away, brought home.'

Like her tidal memory, she was subject to year after year of absence and return, her driftwood suitcases never quite unpacked, never firmly on shore. 'Very upsetting for your family,' I said. The sentiment, well exercised, trotted out mechanically, and earned an equally mechanical response.

'Yes, Doctor.' With a dismissive flick of the scissors she knocked over a primitive little statue on the desk. 'Papa's letters to me were emotional banquets. Away from home, I survived on letters to keep me in touch with a more colourful world. Mine was white as a nurse's apron and paper-thin. At home, I searched for proof that I was loved, not just pitied, that I was a woman, not a symptom.' Her left hand began tapping a hypnotic beat on the file and with her right she waved the scissors like a conductor's baton. 'Thief, spy, eavesdropper I became. Pretending to be unconscious of my actions made it easier for me to steal looks at unfinished letters, unattended diaries, unguarded medical reports. I learned to read between the lines, I could hear the noise my silent Mother poured out in letters to Gabriel and Blunt. People's very *thoughts* were audible to me.'

She lifted off the floor a small, battered suitcase and tipped its contents onto the desk. Page after page slid across to me. 'You mentioned *Gowers*, Doctor?' Glued to her family letters were extracts from his and other neurologists' documents, proof that even the best of us can be misguided; these in turn had been grafted onto wallpaper, cardboard, torn scraps of fabric, then linked by handwritten notes. Scarcely a gap between the words, sentences branched off each other in multi-coloured inks, scurrying like neural forests over the papers, edge to edge and vertically up the sides. 'Read *this!*' she demanded. 'And *this!*' Impossible to read it all; nor did I wish to, conscious of my own mental condition. When I failed to speak, Jenny quoted by heart from those scripted arteries on the desk. She made connections, created a plot, a tragedy, and her ghosts jostled us for space, upsetting my

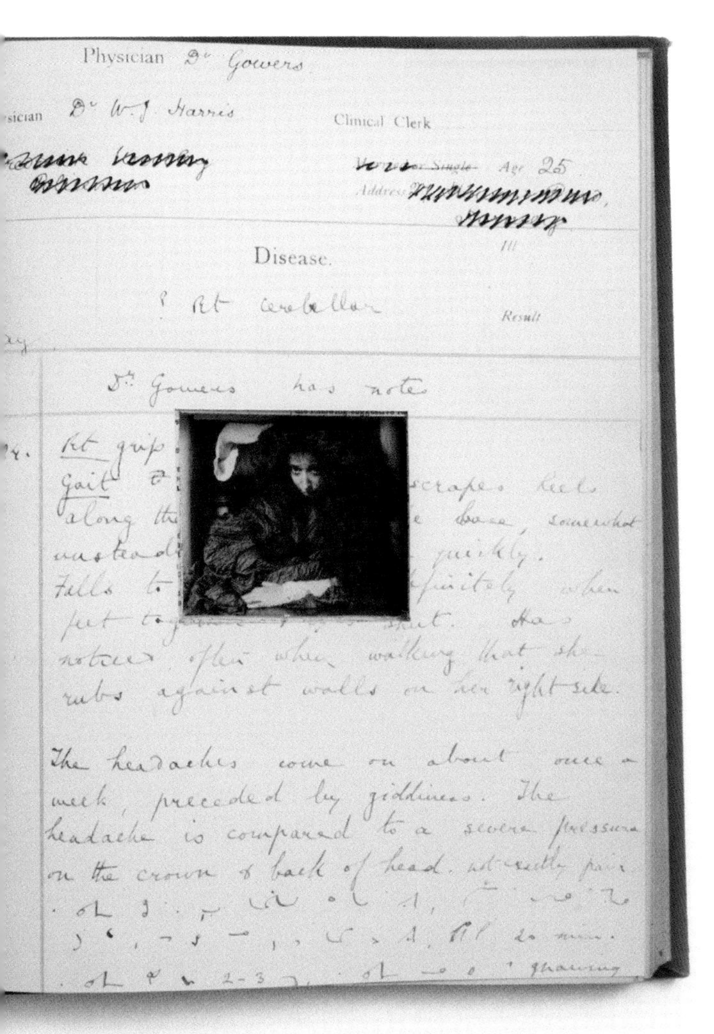
Physician Dr Gowers

Dr W. J. Harris

Clinical Clerk

Single Age 25

Address

Disease.

? Rt cerebellar

Result

Dr Gowers has notes

Rt grip.

Gait scrapes feet along the base, somewhat unsteadi quickly.

Falls to finitely when feet together shut. Has noticed often when walking that she rubs against walls on her right side.

The headaches come on about once a week, preceded by giddiness. The headache is compared to a severe pressure on the crown & back of head.

sense of balance, as if this tiny room were a crowded boat in rough seas. Wave after wave of men and women I had once known flowed through Jenny towards me. Her epileptic brain was generating a thousand ideas too quickly; a thousand neural leaps crossed lobes and hemispheres.

Aware that epileptics can turn, as Van Gogh had done, from manically creative one moment to violent the next, I was on my guard, torn between a desire to escape and a desire to hold Jenny close and stroke her, the way one does a frightened animal. When had she last felt the touch of a hand that was not wielding medicine or needle? For that matter, when had I, a childless, elderly widower, last experienced any more than a handshake? Time was running away from us - unchecked, her electrical storm could soon overwhelm us both.

CHAPTER EIGHT

May's Designs
(translated by an unknown hand)

Because my true feelings are unworthy, I shall confess them only to you, Secret Sketchbook, as if you were a trusted friend. I write in shorthand, which Dr. Gowers' wife taught me, so my thoughts are safe: these squiggly marks I make next to embroidery designs look almost like stitches. 'An artful girl by nature' is what Jenny calls me: we are no longer the JennyandMay that dearest Gabriel sketched at Kelmscott Manor five years ago. I was a child of nine then, his favourite. Now Jenny's illness shrouds our family and he is no longer allowed to stay with us there - the only place in England worth inhabiting, so Jenny insists. The Manor has its ghosts, of course (villagers won't approach it after dark), but they are concerned with their own misfortunes, not ours, and the house too is unconcerned, enclosed by its farm buildings, whose roofs are furry with thatch. 'If we could stroke those roofs,' says Mother, 'I believe they would purr.'

She and I always purred when Gabriel stroked, but Jenny remained somewhat apart, observing our actions with a lawyer's eyes. She wears the same judgemental expression whenever Mother encourages her to lay down a book and take up embroidery (at which I excel). Yesterday, while we sewed, Jenny sang under her breath: *Side by side we sit here stitching, softly softly never speaking of those mother, daughter, father secrets. Silent silky satin Mother, forward one stitch, then another, another. I hope this makes dear mother happier. Makes her chuckle as she used to do in quiet chuckly letters to Gabriel. Mummy put a pansy outside her door when she was ready to beddy him. Rossetti confetti in her tummy.*

'Be quiet!' I said.

'May, don't chastise your sister, it's her illness speaking,' Mother said, but in a weepy, despondent voice. She stood up. 'I'll leave you two alone for a few minutes, so that you can apologise.' So that you can wipe your teary eyes, I thought.

Chastise Jenny and she is capable of spinning herself into a rage as ferocious as Papa's. But that didn't stop me yesterday: 'Look how you've upset Mother, you stupid cow!' There was a long silence. She was staring at me but seemed to be listening to someone else, and then she said, *Call Mother!* She blinked and blinked and her head jerked and she had barely time to lie down. When I touched her wrist, the pulse was beating too fast to count. Her teeth ground audibly, her hands clenched, her breathing grew stertorous and her head was thrown back like Mother's is in Gabriel's paintings. Shudder, shudder she went, back arched, shaken by some tremendous force - an earthquake, a lightning bolt.

It was the nurse's afternoon off. I should have called for help, but I kept quiet, and when Papa arrived home later to roar at us about not protecting Jenny while she was having her fit, I acted innocent and Mother took the blame, without a word or glance of reproach at me. His roaring continued all night. It's not fair! All Jenny has to do these days is grow silent or flash her eyes and they both come running (if Papa is at home, that is, which he isn't much). Are you all right, love? Can we get you a cup of tea? A trip to the seaside? Holidays in a castle? An Italian villa?

'Why can't we visit Gabriel!' I shouted at Mother this morning. 'Why didn't you let him adopt me when he asked? You and Father have Jenny, after all.'

A later page

Papa sends letter after letter with very best love to Darling Jenny, All his love to Dearest Own Jenny. His love is used up on her, barely enough left to offer Mother and me fond wishes and his latest wallpaper designs. Most of his letters to Jenny are signed 'Your loving father, William Morris', but occasionally he is 'Your Old Proosian Blue', a reminder, she insists, that blue is his favourite colour. I must pinch myself to avoid mentioning that Prussian Blue is a synthetic pigment. Resentment is for me a permanent prescription, a bitter medicine I swallow, just as Jenny must swallow bromide. Our poor father. Desperate measures will be needed to prevent her wearing out his heart and poetry for good.

January 16, 1889 **Darling Jenny, Here is the promised letter such as it may turn out; your birthday letter my dear child...hope I shall not have to *write* to you next year.** Therein is a Keats in 4 vols. I know this is a great weight (not upon your conscience, but upon your trunk)... Well darling I must now say good bye. **Your loving father, William Morris**

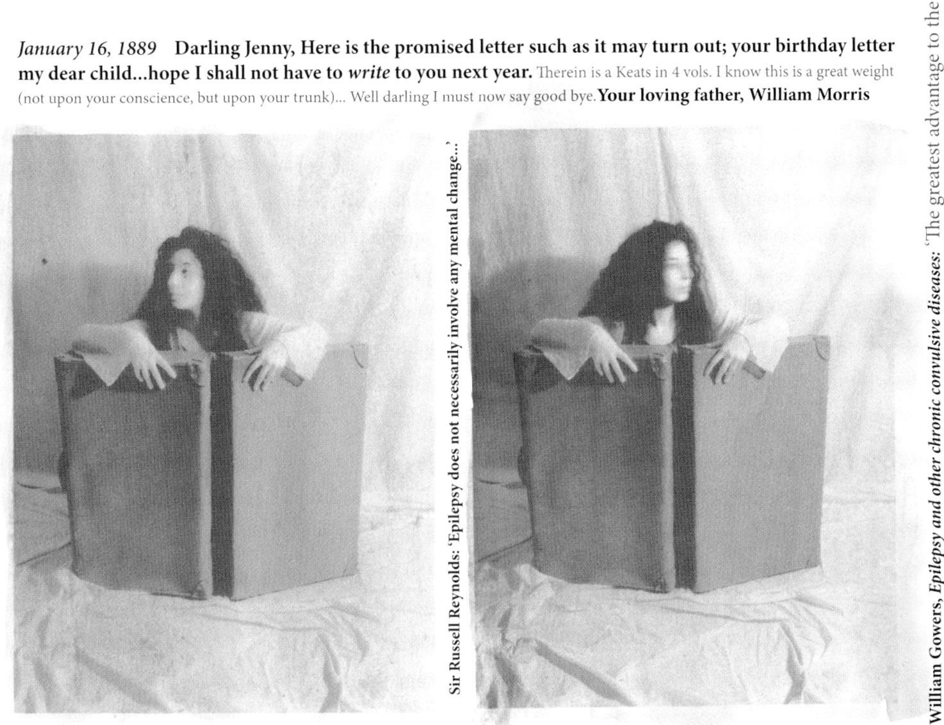

Sir Russell Reynolds: 'Epilepsy does not necessarily involve any mental change...'

January 21, 1889 **Dearest own Jenny, Of course you want to come home and see us my dear child; but I think Mr. Tyrrel is right about your staying on a bit if you can hold out**, though you may think how much I want to see you...Well my darling now I must say good-bye with all my love to you. **Your loving father, William Morris**

Mother to Blunt (*March 17, 1889*): '...came back a few days ago bringing Jenny home...Alas, she is not as well as we hoped for - still she is very much better than she was when she left last autumn...'

February 8, 1889 **I can quite understand your wanting to come home again, and I don't think you ought to be there very much longer at present; but just see how you are at the end of the month...**
On the Monday I lecture to certain art students on Gothic Architecture...**Your loving father, William Morris**

Mother to Mary Howard (*November 1, 1888*): '...grieved that you should have grieved without cause... not the least foundation of truth about our own darling Jenny - on the contrary, she is well and happy with friends at Malvern...'

William Gowers, *Epilepsy and other chronic convulsive diseases*: 'The greatest advantage to the patient results from a complete change of 'moral atmosphere' by removal from home influences, which are often unfavourable by reason of annoyances, or of the unwise solicitude of friends, which fosters instead of controlling the disease...'

Sir Henry Maudsley (*founder of British psychiatry*), *1873*: '...character which the **insane neurosis has in common with the epileptic neurosis is that it is apt to burst out into a convulsive explosion of violence...descendant of an epileptic parent being almost if not quite as likely to become epileptic.'**

CHAPTER NINE

Doctor Q: *Fourth entry*

WITHOUT ANALYSING THE FULL CONSEQUENCES of my action, I stretched my hand out to touch hers, 'May I call you Jenny?'

The manic flow of words slowed and stopped. 'You believe me, then?' she said. 'You find the proof of a conspiracy credible?'

'There is no need to prove yourself to me.'

'But there is *far* more proof than just these few pages! I squirrelled it here, there, everywhere!' She rubbed her browbone, as if summoning a genie to recover a treasure map. 'The trouble is that I forget where those heres and theres are. Pure accident that this old suitcase of mine was found in the attics at Kelmscott Manor. By a cleaner. She has promised not to inform my sister, who would surely take it from me, as she has so many letters and things of mine. For safekeeping, she says, as if I am not safe with my own history. Years she spent diligently gathering Papa's correspondence, then duly published an edition of the letters he wrote. Those letters she approved of, that is, which included only one hundred and fifty of the many he sent me. Her preface to the collection explains that she hesitated over publishing even them, but felt that the world should be permitted a glimpse of their paternal tenderness. She has kept the letters he wrote to me. And when I asked about the ones *I* wrote to *him*, she claimed they had disappeared. *All* of them? What of the letters Mother wrote to me and Papa? "Disappeared as well". How can I believe her? So many lies she tells! According to her, my confinements in nursing homes were always brief. Yet in this suitcase are letters Papa and Mother wrote which prove that one confinement - at Great Malvern - lasted from August 1888 to March 1889.'

Closer and closer we edged towards revelations that I feared to give.

She rubbed her brow again. 'A few weeks home in October, I think, but I have no clear recollection. Best leave your recollections alone, May says, but I would prefer to keep them company. From Papa's letters to me, the ones she published, it's clear that he and I exchanged views on women's suffrage and Marx and...' Tugging loose a strand of her hair, she wound it round the scissors the way Etta used to wind wool. 'I supported the Socialist League Papa formed with Marx's daughter Eleanor and and... those others.' More names lost, more strands of hair unrolled, her scalp now visible. 'I carried the Socialist banner to impoverished neighbourhoods, and heard Papa, defender of the common man, suffer oaths from public house habitués. You can see me in photographs of the League, dead centre.' *Etta just out of the frame. Dead storage.* 'But without my letters to Papa, I am a canvas embroidered by other people, the invalid invalidated. Not even my childhood friends understand my need to remember. They positively discourage it. Useless to solicit information from Papa's biographer Jack Mackail, although his two volumes about my father are deemed "authorative".'

Described to me by Mackail as 'unpleasantly near untruthfulness'.

'In his book Mother, May and I appear as little more than footnotes. Are there no aspects of Papa that our letters would illuminate?'

'I mean no offence, but a complete biography -'

'You judge women's views of Great Men, "Men of Letters", irrelevant?'

'Not in the least, but permit me to say -'

'I copied the letter that a close friend received from Mackail. It went like this: "The fluctuations of illness are no matter for public record. One source of embarrassment in Morris's intimate letters is the perpetual recurrence of Jenny's health." In fact my very existence, perpetually recurring, is an embarrassment, Doctor. The word "epilepsy" appears nowhere in Mackail's book. I am simply the daughter whose health "broke completely down", recipient of her father's "unceasing thought". Papa's "chosen companion".' Pulling the scissors free of her hair, she lay them beside the toppled statuette.

It glared at me: Admit! Confess! But I veered off at a tangent once again. 'My field of expertise is not epilepsy,' I said, 'it is the cerebral trauma which leads to speechlessness and loss of voice: "aphasia" and "aphonia". Both can be triggered by hysteria.'

'Aphasia, aphonia, hysteria. They sound like a trio of music hall performers. Ladies and Gentlemen, may I present to you the Three Fates, Three Furies, Three Harpies. Three Graces need not apply. Only a furious

harpy can hold out against the conspiring doctors. They prefer me silent.'

Up and down went her emotions, and my pulse followed, hammering dangerously. 'Why would any doctor conspire against his patient?'

'To hide his own errors of judgement?'

Could speechlessness be judged a crime? There was I, an encyclopaedia of voice pathologies, suffering from an absence of the will to speak out. My brain conspired against itself; I found only platitudes to offer Jenny. They did, however, settle her brain enough that I felt safe to ask why she believed private family letters might be found at this hospital.

'I am playing Sherlock Holmes, Doctor. In my possession is a letter of March 1878, written by Papa to Mother when she was with me in Italy. He mentions two epilepsy specialists from here who were involved with my treatment: Charles Bland Radcliffe, a friend and physician to the Burne-Jones family.' She had to allow her memory to catch up. 'And John Russell Reynolds. Rather keen on the benefits of electricity, wasn't he?'

'I believe that both men had their patients' best interests at heart.' A half-truth, for in my opinion both men were *over* keen on applying electricity to treat loss of speech. Never liked Radcliffe. Had he achieved his aims, this hospital would have taken a decidedly commercial turn. First and foremost I was a disciple of Hughlings Jackson and Gowers. Jackson, that philosopher-physician, envisioned cathedrals of the brain; Gowers supplied the cathedral's bricks and mortar, reviewing thousands of cases for what has become our Bible of neurological diseases. Three times a week he would sit at the patients' bedsides, re-read their casenotes and then, after meticulous examinations, elaborate on diagnoses made by other clinicians. Gowers, whose insistence on tracing symptoms to their origin earned him the nickname 'Primary Lesion', would have appreciated Jenny's tenacious pursuit of Truth. But I had grown weary. 'Try playing Holmes in these archives,' I said, 'and you will require an archaelogist, not a Watson. As for Reynolds, he resigned from active staff here in 1869, and at any rate would have treated you privately: this hospital wasn't intended for well-off patients.' Or incurables. Brimming with philanthropy we were, but Reynolds insisted that treatment was the key: *'Treatment, treatment, treatment, always treatment!'* As numbers of patients grew, so did our scientific knowledge, and daily routine became a well-oiled machinery to match our industrial era. When our efforts to cure failed, it was because we strove for miracles. Patients judged untreatable by the Board were replaced by more hopeful cases. The Discharged might be treated in the Outpatient department, but must be cared for elsewhere.

One soldier checked himself out voluntarily. I try to forget his reasons.

'January 29, 1917: This is to certify that I have decided to discharge myself from the National Hospital for Paralysed and Epileptic because I am afraid to undergo the treatment which proved beneficial to me on a previous occasion. I take full responsibility for what may happen to me after I leave.'

Please, Jenny, don't remember the beneficial treatments you underwent. Wherever they were done (not here, I pray), discharge yourself. She was regarding me closely. 'Something about you, Doctor - have we met before?'

'Never.'

'You are certain?' She moved around the desk towards me. Uneasy, I retreated to the opposite side. Now I faced the books and she the pictures. Again she circled towards me, again I retreated. Logic, emotion, logic, emotion. She played her fingers along the books, pressing titles as if they were piano keys. 'Not here?'

'My neurological papers are widely circulated.'

'Such measured tones. Is your whole life measured out drip by drip, like medicine? I would have thought that you would be more understanding of my situation. Are we not alike? You are half-caste, I am half-castaway.'

Taken aback, quite literally, I had to steady myself against the wall, and its flowery pattern metamorphosed into a jungle before my eyes, turning a venomous green. 'Colour is not the issue here,' I forced out.

'Prejudice is always an issue, Doctor.'

Indeed. The very mention of racial origins can still pierce my tawny mind; an unwarranted sensitivity, for even during those years when England was still trading goods with slave-owners in America, at Queen Square there had been doctors of mixed race working beside white. My career has been unhindered by the few shabby souls who described me having 'fuzzy-wuzzy' hair and complexion. How Etta mocked those men! Whiter than white, she expressed pleasure at the way black chooses to dye my skin. Across the dark

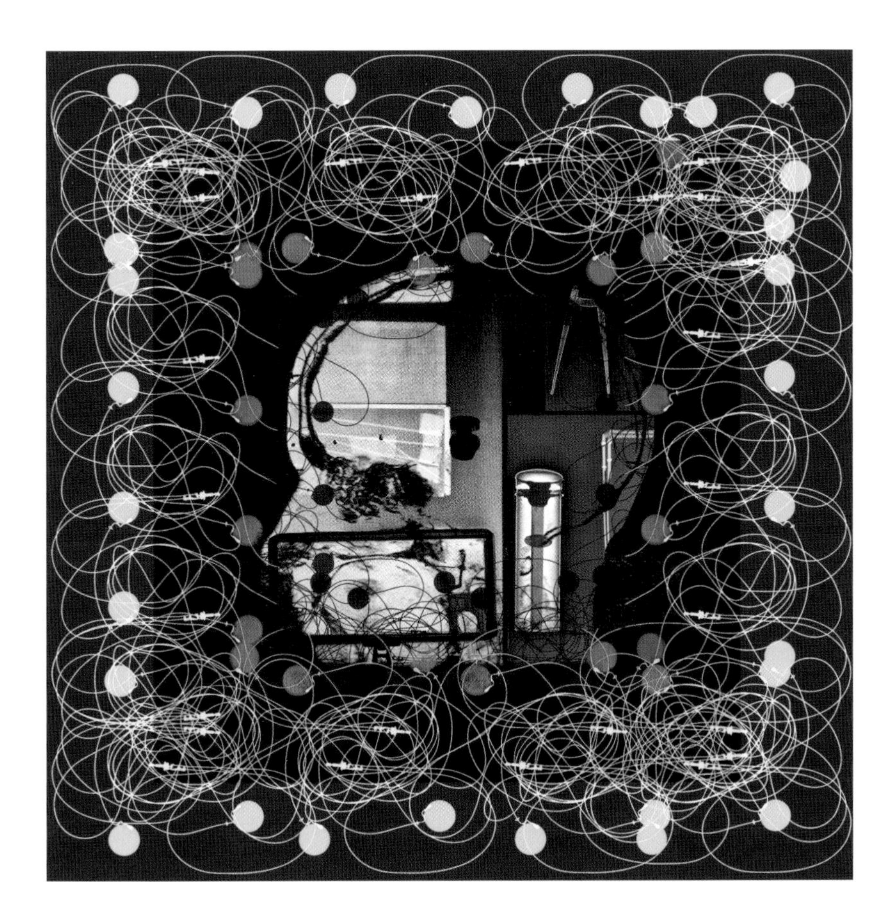

pools of my groin she would run her fingers, encircling me the way one does a champagne flute. 'Here's to Mauritius, this lush island east of Madagascar,' she said, 'held by the Dutch, the French, the British - and now by me.' Gripping me in her hand. 'Volcanic in origins, a fertile soil where tropical cyclones often occur.' She dissuaded me from flattening my hair with pommade. 'Its wanton and disobedient nature is another side of you that remains Mauritian, defying empires.'

Jenny intruded on Etta's ghost. 'I still believe we must have met.'

'I can only re-affirm that we have not.' Not in the sense she was referring to; that much is true. The last time we had been this close was the summer of 1889, when she was stretched out unconscious on a hospital bed. The procedure she had endured there had been for her own good, the surgeon insisted. 'Her condition was life-threatening.'

Whose life was threatened, though? Whose lives?

UNDER the WALLPAPER

by Leslie Forbes

'The history of epilepsy can be summarised as 4000 years of ignorance, superstition and stigma, followed by 100 years of knowledge, superstition and stigma.'

Rajendra Kale, *Bringing Epilepsy Out of the Shadows* (British Medical Journal, 1997)

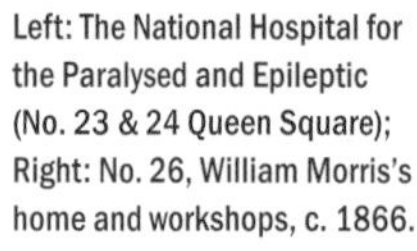

Left: The National Hospital for the Paralysed and Epileptic (No. 23 & 24 Queen Square); Right: No. 26, William Morris's home and workshops, c. 1866.

'Queen Square, Bloomsbury, is a little enclosure of tall trees and comely old brick houses...It seems to have been set apart for the humanities of life and the alleviation of all hard destinies... As you go round it, you read, upon every second door-plate, some offer of help to the afflicted...'
Robert Louis Stevenson

Collaboration

This book (first of four parts) is integral to the project titled *Embroidered Minds*, where artists, writers, doctors and historians explore the ways, positive and negative, that epilepsy could have affected the Morris family, and still affects families today. As well as the novel, our project includes a series of exhibitions linked to it but adapted to reflect places in which they are shown. Inspired by real objects and people associated with the Morris circle, the exhibitions allow us a wider range of opportunities to engage with the public. Publishing the printed novel in serial form, with new chapters, ongoing commentaries and art developed further on our website, is a nod at the Victorian tradition used for the works of William Morris, Charles Dickens, H.G. Wells and Wilkie Collins (among many others), whose stories, first serialised in magazines, were subsequently adapted to be printed as books.

Women in the Square

It was the mystery of Jenny's and Jane's missing letters that started me writing a novel, but as I searched for links between William Morris's letters and Jenny's epilepsy, I was struck by the question of why no Morris historians gave the National Hospital for Paralysis and Epilepsy more than a passing reference, or flagged up the family's unavoidable association with Queen Square's neurological circle, where women played an important role. In fact, the National Hospital owes its existence not to science but to the Chandler sisters and their brother. An ordinary Victorian family of modest means, the Chandlers had watched their grandmother die, paralysed, without being able to help her. At that time, the mid 19th-century, no medical establishments were specifically devoted to treating neurological conditions such as paralysis and epilepsy. Determined to change the situation, the Chandlers used what influence they had to raise financial assistance, and in 1860 a small neurological hospital was founded at No. 24 Queen Square. A year after Morris arrived at No. 26, the National Hospital had gained sufficient support to expand its premises into No. 23.

In Queen Square during the Morrises' time, boundaries - medical, political and artistic - were being crossed, between men's and women's roles in particular. There were anomalies, of course: William Gowers, whose father made ladies' boots, was entirely opposed to women becoming doctors, whereas his associate Victor Horsley, born into privilege, applauded women's suffrage, a cause that Jane Morris was ambivalent about. And Horsley's younger brother Gerald, devoted acolyte of her husband, founded the Art Worker's Guild, which wouldn't allow women to join (and even today refers to its women members as 'Brothers').

Poor Exile: the real Jenny Morris

'...there is a region in which we must recognise hypothesis as absolute, the region below the surface whence no reflected light can pass, but whence all observed phenomena proceed.'
William Gowers
The Dynamics of Life, 1894

Where do history and story diverge?

Passages in the story I've written are direct responses to the collaborating artists' work rather than to history, a 'novel' method for me. Still, *Embroidered Minds of the Morris Women* is not about what *did* happen to Jenny, but what *might* have. The enigmatic Dr. Q is entirely fictional, but the doctors he mentions did practice at Queen Square. The letters on pages 47 and 55 are extracts from real documents; the chapters by Jane Morris were 'imagined' by the biographer Jan Marsh. Several photographs in the book are of real Morris women, most of them are not. The wallpapered hospital room where Jenny confronts Dr. Q doesn't exist. However, part of Queen Square's vast, world-renowned National Hospital for Neurology and Neurosurgery includes a Victorian building called the Powis Wing, and on the walls of its 19th-century Boardroom is Morris-patterned wallpaper. Built in 1882, after Morris's workshops and the original hospital were knocked down, the Powis Wing is where my epilepsy is treated by a neurologist who accepts that if I took enough drugs to stop all my seizures, I couldn't write. I choose to take the minimum number of pills and keep writing.

The National Hospital for the Paralysed and Epileptic
(now called the Powis Wing)

Happy Endings

In *Epilepsy: Perception, Imagination and Change* Jim Chambliss of Melbourne Medical School looks at how exceptionally active the human brain is when in a defocussed, manic or chaotic state (such as that caused by certain kinds of epileptic seizures): its neuronal activity more free-flowing, more able to make unusual connections and forge new ideas. Not many people imagine the epileptic condition producing creative results. Dr. Renata Whurr has joked that she likes happy endings: 'With a novel like "Embroidered Minds of the Morris Women" - and I don't read novels, only textbooks, even before I go to sleep, a happy ending for me would be if through this work, society became more aware, more accepting about epilepsy than it used to be.'

'Science - we have loved her well, and followed her diligently, what will she do? I feel she is so much in the pay of the counting house...'
William Morris
The Decorative Arts: Lecture to the Trades Guild, 1877

CONTRIBUTORS

JULIA DWYER lectures in interior architecture at the University of Westminster and Chelsea College of Arts, and has participated in a number of collaborative public art and design projects over the past decade.

LESLIE FORBES is the award-winning writer of 4 novels and many BBC Radio series, and author/illustrator of 4 travel books. Since 1997 she has been collaborating on projects with scientists and fine artists.

CAROLINE ISGAR is an artist known for her prints and artist's book collaborations, including *The Secret Staircase* for the Foundling Museum. She is an Art Workers' Guild member and a former printmaking Research Fellow at the Slade School of Fine Art.
www.carolineisgar.co.uk

DR. MARJORIE LORCH is Professor of Neurolinguistics at Birkbeck, University of London. Her interdisciplinary research focusses on how language is represented in the brain using clinical, experimental and historical approaches.
www.bbk.ac.uk/linguistics/our-staff/academic-staff/marjorie-lorch

JAN MARSH is a biographer and curator, author of *Pre-Raphaelite Sisterhood* and *Jane & May Morris*, co-editor of the *Collected Letters of Jane Morris*, curator of *Black Victorians*, and current president of the William Morris Society. janmarsh.blogspot.com

SUE RIDGE is an artist, curator and lecturer in Fine Art at Chelsea College of Arts. Most of her artwork has been made in and for public and institutional spaces, recently focussing on issues involving hospital environments. www.sueridge.com

ANDREW THOMAS is a graphic designer who works in print, branding and exhibition design for a wide range of clients including major museums, commercial companies and charities.

DR. RENATA WHURR is an academic, researcher and therapist whose expertise is in dealing with patients suffering from communication problems related to neurological speech, voice and language disorders.

With thanks to these individuals and organisations for their support:
Nina Saeidi, who helped discover our 'lost' Morris women | Queen Square Archives Committee |
Sarah Lawson,Librarian, Queen Square Library, Archive & Museum | Anna Mason, William Morris Gallery |
The William Morris Society |Gemma Lewis - A+E Superintendant Radiographer, University College Hospitals NHS Foundation Trust (UCLH) | University of the Arts - CCW Print Services | Margarita Kovnat, Markov Print, Digital Textile Printing | Professor Rosemary Ashton |
We gratefully acknowledge the support of the Gowers family.

Picture Credits

Dust Jacket & Cover Fabric printed with *Aphasia Wallpaper* © Sue Ridge; Photography - Andrew Thomas | **P4** Etching © Caroline Isgar | **P7-9** Images of Nina Saiedi - Andrew Thomas | **P10-11** Collage images from Research Sketchbook © Sue Ridge | **P13** Map - Andrew Thomas; Map of Queen Square projected onto Nina Saeidi © Sue Ridge & Julia Dwyer | **P14** *Post seizure Pre-Raphaelite Dress* © Leslie Forbes; *Wilted Tulips Wallpaper pattern* © Sue Ridge; Photograph - Andrew Thomas |**P17** *Aphasia Wallpaper detail with Mugwort* © Sue Ridge | **P18** Etching © Caroline Isgar | **P21** *Nerves & Flowers* © Sue Ridge; *May Morris; Margaret Mackail (née Burne-Jones); Sir Philip Burne-Jones, 2nd Bt; Jane Alice ('Jenny') Morris by Frederick Holyer* © National Portrait Gallery, London | **P24** *May Morris* by Unknown photographer © National Portrait Gallery, London; *Blood supply to the central ganglia* from William Gowers collection © Queen Square Library, Archive & Museum; Map from *Epping Forest* by Edward North Buxton | **P26-27** *Jenny Morris* by Unknown photographer © William Morris Gallery, London; Photograph - Andrew Thomas | **P28** Photograph of Nina Saiedi - Andrew Thomas| **P31** *Ceramic Memory Box* © Andrew Thomas | **P32** Etching © Caroline Isgar | **P34-35** Photographs of Nina Saiedi - Andrew Thomas | **P38** *Morris Warp Scan Wallpaper* © Sue Ridge | **P39** Drawing from William Gowers collection © Queen Square Library, Archive & Museum | **P40** Etching © Caroline Isgar | **P45** *Jane Morris (née Burden)* by Robert Faulkener & Co © National Portrait Gallery, London; image of Nina Saiedi with EEG pattern © Andrew Thomas | **P48** Photographic collage © Andrew Thomas | **P50-51** *Casenotes* (page from *News from Nowhere* by William Morris, William Gowers casenote page © Queen Square Library, Archive & Museum) © Andrew Thomas | **P52** Etching © Caroline Isgar | **P55** Images © Leslie Forbes | **P58** *Epileptic Wallpaper with Wires* © Sue Ridge; *Epileptic Wallpaper* projected onto Nina Saeidi © Sue Ridge & Julia Dwyer | **P61** *Leslie's Brain with Electrode Wires* © Sue Ridge | **P62** *The Hospital in Queen Square 1866* © UCL Institute of Neurology; *William Morris's House* © Queen Square Library, Archive & Museum | **P63** *Jane Alice ('Jenny') Morris* by Unknown photographer © National Portrait Gallery, London | **P63** Postcard *National Hospital Facade* © Queen Square Library, Archive & Museum

Printed in Great Britain
by Amazon